Warwickshire County Council

This item is to be returned or renewed before the latest date above. It may be borrowed for a further period if not in demand. **To renew your books:**

- **Phone the 24/7 Renewal Line 01926 499273 or**
- **Visit www.warwickshire.gov.uk/libraries**

Discover • Imagine • Learn • *with libraries*

Warwickshire County Council

Working for Warwickshire

PROOF OF
THEIR SIN

PROOF OF THEIR SIN

BY

DANI COLLINS

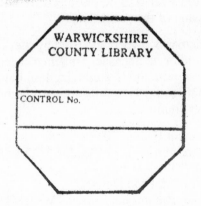

MILLS
BOON®

First published in Great Britain 2013
by Mills & Boon, an imprint of Harlequin (UK) Limited.
Large Print edition 2013
Harlequin (UK) Limited, Eton House,
18-24 Paradise Road, Richmond, Surrey TW9 1SR

© Dani Collins 2013

ISBN: 978 0 263 23236 3

Harlequin (UK) policy is to use papers that are natural,
renewable and recyclable products and made from
wood grown in sustainable forests. The logging and
manufacturing process conform to the legal environmental
regulations of the country of origin.

Printed and bound in Great Britain
by CPI Antony Rowe, Chippenham, Wiltshire

Happy Twentieth Anniversary to my love, my husband Doug. (A bit late, but publishing doesn't happen overnight, honey. Just like a marriage.)

A loving thank you to my mother, Sharon, for leaving her Janet Dailey books on the coffee table when I was in high school. Yes, this book in your hands is all your fault.

However, Mom does share credit with the editors at Harlequin London—most especially Suzy Clarke for her initial encouragement and my current editor, Megan Haslam, for the spot-on coaching that make my stories bigger, better, stronger.

I'd like to also wish a Happy First Anniversary to Sandra and Dave. This is how you get a man to buy a romance novel for his wife, people. Dave will do it. He's a romantic and a gentleman.

And a very affectionate acknowledgement of my fellow author Cathryn Parry, who has been the most supportive friend you can imagine. If the planets align, I'll hand this to you in person.

CHAPTER ONE

NOT FOR THE first time in the last several weeks, Lauren Bradley wondered where she should draw the line between becoming the bold, independent woman she'd always wished she could be and behaving like a shameless, demanding radical. Words like *licentious, brazen* and *embarrassment* trickled through her mind with increasing frequency as she walked that blurry border.

Unsurprisingly, when those hurtful words echoed in her head, they were always pronounced in her mother's thin, distressed voice.

Flicking one long, brunette braid over her shoulder, Lauren silently told her absent mother to pipe down while she regarded the woman behind the counter of this exclusive hotel salon. The woman had just given Lauren the most excruciatingly polite brush-off and the habits of a lifetime urged Lauren to slink away in quiet disgrace.

But her heart was beating for two these days,

knocking hard against the wall of her breastbone and bouncing back on a spine that had to harden to contain it.

Dare I? she wondered with a shiver of apprehension.

Oh, she knew she appeared to be just one more hick tourist come to New York looking for a posh hairstyle to take home as a souvenir, but this meant so much more to her than that. Lauren stood on the threshold of taking control of her life in a way she'd never imagined, but to do so meant shoving past the old Lauren who always smilingly took a backseat to everyone. If she didn't dig deep and find her true spirit right now she might as well collect her luggage from upstairs and retreat to the empty rooms of her grandmother's mansion where she could raise her baby with all the fear of drawing attention its mother had suffered most of her life.

No. Lauren locked her knee, surreptitiously putting her foot down.

She allowed the salon receptionist to finish the call she'd used to try to dismiss her. Ingrained manners were a pain that way. Besides, Lauren needed the extra seconds to gather her courage and manufacture a gracious smile for the woman who gave her a strained *Still here?* smile as she hung up.

"I believe there's been a miscommunication," Lauren said with the most warmly modulated yet implacable tone she could muster. "I'm attending the Donatelli Charity Ball this evening."

The woman, a little younger than Lauren's nearly twenty-five, widened her eyelash extensions with a fraction of respect. *Exactly.* Paolo Donatelli was a man who made every woman stand taller and suck in her stomach.

A zing of empowerment swept through Lauren. She was name-dropping, sure, but she'd never before had the gall to try it. Over her mother's gasp of horror, she heard her grandmother say, *Good girl!* Clenching her fingers on the strap of her carry-all purse, Lauren added daringly, "You're certain you have nothing for Bradley? Mrs. Ryan Bradley?"

Her mother would have a stroke over such audacity, but Lauren stood her ground, pronouncing the name with delicate precision because, honestly, what was the use in *being* Mrs. Bradley if she shrank from all it afforded her?

"Mrs. Bradley..." The salon hostess searched

her book while her plucked brows came together in concern. "It sounds familiar—"

A stiletto-thin man appeared from behind the privacy wall of translucent bricks. Groomed to perfection right down to his buffed fingernails, he greeted Lauren with the warmth of an old friend, even though she'd never seen him before in her life.

"Mrs. Bradley, of course we have time for you. So good to see you out during what must be a very difficult time. May I express on behalf of myself, my staff, and in fact our entire country, how sincerely sorry we are for your loss. Captain Bradley was a true hero. If there is anything we can do to ease your pain and make up for his sacrifice, we are at your service."

Now Lauren did feel like the most conscience-less snake oil salesman in the world, allowing the man to sweep her into the interior of the salon, minions scampering before him to remove traces of previous clients.

Guilt rose to tense her shoulders; there was still time to go back. All she had to do was turn and leave. People would stare but she could be gone in a matter of seconds.

She swallowed and allowed confident hands to

seat her. The elastic hoops were peeled off her two thick braids and then her new BFF was fanning his hands through her hair, picking up the strands that fell to her waist.

"This is your natural color, isn't it? What a treasure. Your husband must have adored this mane."

Lauren had thought he had adored her. *Don't ever cut it. Promise me,* he'd said a thousand times. Everyone in her life had encouraged her to keep her hair long and Lauren, always the good girl, had complied.

"You're not going to hide it by putting it up? What are you wearing tonight?" He weighed the kinked strands.

"I have a vintage Lanvin-Castillo. And no, I don't want my hair up. I want you to cut it. Off." New life. New Lauren.

He sucked in a gasp, meeting her gaze in the mirror with disbelief that slowly dawned into awe. "My dear, if I were straight, I would ask you to marry me."

Lauren smiled as if men fell for her all the time, which was the furthest thing from the truth. "Sir, if I was the least bit interested in marrying again, I'd say yes."

* * *

Three hours later Enrique was the best friend Lauren had never had. He insisted on coming to her room with one of the stylists from his salon where they helped her dress and put finishing touches on her hair, nails and makeup.

"I cannot wait to tell people I dressed Frances Hammond's granddaughter. Look at you! It's like it was made for you."

Considering it was the last dress made for her grandmother and that she'd also been three months' pregnant at the time, it didn't surprise Lauren that it fit so well. The boned bodice that flattened her tender breasts was severely uncomfortable, but it did wonders for her usually modest bosom. She hid her wince and stepped into the matching satin heels. They weren't as tall as current fashion dictated, but they were stitched to match the amethyst embroidery on the white silk of the dress and positively adorable.

Enrique carefully draped the dark violet stole over her bare shoulders, shaking his head with wonder. "Look at this detailing. What a time to be alive." He set familiar hands on her hips, taking in the pink and blue pastes studding the elaborate chenille and floss that ended at her waistline. He didn't seem to notice she was disguising a pregnancy behind the structure of the dress.

Good. The whole purpose of this exercise was to let the father of her baby know about his child's existence before the rest of the world found out.

As Lauren absorbed the reality that she would be seeing Paolo again, a flood of excitement sent a subtle rush of heat and color under her skin. She saw it happen in the full-length mirror as she turned for a final look. It made her squirm internally with chagrin that she couldn't stop the reaction. Always, always she reacted to that man and it was so wrong. Her thoughts of him almost tipped into memories of their night in Charleston and the sting in her cheeks ached with shame.

She tried forcing herself back into the cone of denial she'd occupied since The Morning After, but it was tighter than this dress. The lovemaking shouldn't have happened, but it had. There were consequences. She had to face them.

Which meant facing Paolo.

To combat her reaction at the prospect of seeing him, she took a hard look at her appearance. Where her grandmother had been blond elegance,

Lauren was dark with elfin features accentuated by her new hair.

What would Paolo think? Of the hair and the news?

She never knew what to expect from him. The first time she'd met him, at a bar here in New York five years ago, he'd been warm and admiring. The second time, at her wedding to Ryan half a year later, things had gone so wrong it had been nothing but chilly brush-offs after that. She'd been convinced he hated her and, after his nasty set-down at Ryan's thirtieth birthday party, she had returned his antipathy. When Ryan had disappeared three months ago, however, she'd made one despairing call from Charleston and Paolo had materialized before her. He'd revealed an incredibly tender side when he'd broken the news about Ryan with sincere regret, so protective of her he had whisked her to the privacy of his nearby penthouse.

Where he had made love to her with unexpected and abject passion.

So would he regard this baby as exciting and wonderful? Or would he be the iceman about it? Would he blame her? Or see her as something he wanted?

Oh God, was that what she was doing? Trying to make herself into something that could fit into his world? Suddenly she saw herself as she was: a rube playing dress-up, sidling out of her element with the intention of taking life by storm without possessing the capacity to actually do it. Her confidence plunged.

"Don't look so terrified," Enrique scolded. "You have every reason to hold your head high."

Lauren couldn't think of one person who would agree. Not her mother, certainly not her mother-in-law. Paolo hadn't said a word to her since. That didn't bode well.

Her stomach rolled with anxious fear and she automatically lifted a protective hand to her abdomen.

Enrique's gaze followed.

Too revealing. She was falling apart.

"I haven't eaten," she offered, which was true. The baby deserved better. She ought to take off this costume and stay here for a proper meal and an early night.

"They'll have a buffet at the ball, but will this tide you over?" Enrique's assistant offered a candy from a roll of them.

Lauren stared with bemusement at that particular candy appearing before her at this particular instance. With a tremulous smile, she took one. As the O-shape and scorched-caramel flavor landed on her tongue, Mamie's spirit came into the room.

Do it, chérie. *Take a chance. Live your life.*

Lauren took a deep breath and her flagging confidence rallied. She couldn't let Mamie down.

She secured the antique earrings weighing down her lobes then adjusted her grandmother's diamonds across her collarbone and, with all the terrified dignity of Marie Antoinette approaching the guillotine, made her way to the Grand Ballroom.

Paolo Donatelli surveyed the charity benefit his mother had begun hosting on an annual basis when his father had still been alive. Whichever country they happened to occupy in December became the location of a White Tie Ball complete with full orchestra, champagne fountains and a midnight supper. The Donatellis could then retreat to Italy for a family Christmas confident they'd done their duty by the local economy, their position in society, and the cause du jour.

His mother rarely left home in winter these days,

but Paolo strove to do her credit by continuing the tradition abroad. In his hypercritical opinion, he'd pulled off one of the most successful events to date. If there was a flaw, it was the lack of a proper wife to be his hostess, not that anyone would dare say so. If his cousin Vittorio had an opinion on the subject, he wisely kept it to himself. And Paolo was working on repairing that deficiency. Isabella Nutini was his companion tonight and she was nothing if not proper.

He nodded an acknowledgment when Isabella excused herself to the powder room, thinking she could easily repair more than one blemish in his life. She was Italian, not one of these mixed-breed Americans as his first wife had been. Isabella had been raised Catholic and so treated marriage with the respect it deserved. She seemed to have a grasp on concepts such as loyalty and duty to family— something he saw in very few people these days, man or woman.

Best of all, aside from the requisite level of physical attraction and a modicum of intellectual interest, he felt little for her. He was a man of very deep emotions and controlling them was a daily struggle. Best to have a wife who wouldn't put him through an emotional wringer. As long as she provided him the children he required and did not shame him before his family, Isabella was ideal.

"Your date left you and now so will I," Vittorio said with cheerful insolence. "Excuse me, cousin, while I seduce my future wife."

Italian heritage and male curiosity demanded Paolo catch a glimpse of the female that had drawn another man's interest. He turned his head and—

A pendulum of suppressed sexual need that he'd pushed far into his subconscious swung through him and exploded, nearly bringing him to his knees in a rush of heat and primitive hunger. Paolo slapped his hand onto the ruffled front of Vittorio's shirt, freezing him in place. Iron hardened in his arm while his gaze swept like a raptor, ensuring no one else dared approach her before he locked onto her again and took in the vision of her.

She'd gained back a few pounds, but her cheekbones still stood out under eyes that were wide and overwhelmed as she searched the crowd. Despite her height, she projected an intrinsic vulnerability that struck him the way it had when he'd entered the house of Ryan Bradley's family in Charleston. His protective instincts rose like hackles, but she wasn't nearly as helpless as she appeared. Lauren Bradley knew how to take care of herself. Like most women, she turned on the damsel-in-distress act to get what she wanted.

Ryan has disappeared, Paolo. No one will tell me anything. Please help me.

She had known how to get right at his heart, plucking at his deep allegiance to his friend despite playing them off against each other for years. With one phone message, she'd invited him onto an emotional roller coaster that had taken him weeks to recover from. A man in his position couldn't afford inner turmoil. She ought to understand and respect that, but she was too self-involved.

Dio! She was beautiful, though. He vaguely took in a dress of white silk swirled with pearlescent design. A slash of dark purple was tangled over creamy shoulders and pale arms, but his gaze ate up the other details: the swell of her pale breasts, the hourglass shape nipped at the waist and flared to wide hips that had cradled his like they'd been made to lock together the way they had. Her neck had been a slender arch under his rapacious mouth, her ears so sensitive his breath on them had made her quiver. And those lips, those plump, edible lips had roamed his chest and abdomen and—

"Are you forgetting you brought a date, Paolo?" Vittorio's voice held the same amused mockery Paolo had heard all too often from family after his marriage had fallen apart. *How could you not have suspected it wasn't yours?*

Lauren Bradley had the ability to make him miss certain things and overlook the rest. Shame rose to burn his cheeks, mixed with embarrassment and anger. She'd seduced him into another dishonorable position and he would never forgive her for it.

"That's Mrs. Bradley. Off-limits. To everyone," he ground out, finally dropping the hand that had warded off his cousin. *"Scusa,"* he added from between clenched teeth, loathe to approach her, but what choice did he have?

Vittorio flicked him a speculative glance. Paolo ignored it, admitting to nothing. Everyone had wanted to know what had happened when he had stolen Lauren from the Bradley household and taken her to his penthouse on top of the Donatelli Bank Tower in Charleston.

Nothing, he'd lied.

He never lied, especially to family. Lauren had

brought him to this level of disgrace and now she had the nerve to turn up at the grandest event his family sponsored. To gloat? To push him a few rungs lower than he already stood in his own estimation? Where did she find the audacity to dress like royalty and parade herself into public barely three months into mourning a man regarded by the nation as a saint?

Her searching gaze found him, causing an unwanted zing of electric excitement to pierce him. Instantly he was transported to the darkened bedroom and the rumpled bed. He felt again the ever-expanding brush of skin on skin as they struggled to peel away each other's clothing, neither willing to break the kiss or stop touching the other. His blood heated and a weighted sensation tugged in his groin. Everything he'd suppressed and forced himself to forget rushed back with renewed power, exalting him with a conqueror's strength and spirit even as it sickened him to want her like this.

Unceasingly. Uncontrollably.

While on her side, her plumped breasts rose as she caught and held her breath. Her shiny lips parted. She was a precocious little Bambi, wide-eyed and pinned by what looked like apprehension, so damned defenseless-looking, but it was an act. A trick to trip him up and bring him to heel. She wanted something and he wouldn't like it, that he was sure of.

They moved toward each other like drifting flotsam pushed by a tide then halted. He was able to see the subtle things now. The uncertainty trembling in her thick lashes, the way she forced her chin up because facing him wasn't easy. *Good.* She ought to be burning in self-hatred the way he had been doing since betraying his personal code and his closest friend.

She lifted a hand in a way he'd surreptitiously watched her do a hundred times, but there was no tendril to tuck behind her ear. *Dio!* He should have noticed it first, not last.

"What the hell have you done to your hair?" he growled.

Lauren self-consciously touched the fine wisps Enrique had left against her neck, habitually about to apologize for daring to think she had the right to cut her own hair.

Fortunately she was too dazzled by the sight of Paolo to speak at all. He was not a man who needed a white tuxedo to impress, but the one he wore added elegance and power to an already gorgeous man. His hair was on the darker side of brown, thick and threatening to curl. His olive skin held the remnants of a warm, summer tan. Beneath it, his face was carved in lines of supreme masculine grace, handsome without being pretty, strong to the point of ruggedness, but polished to urbane sophistication. He'd mastered aloof detachment but had every ounce of the seductively expressive eyes of his heritage.

Those eyes had been flipping her heart since the first time she'd seen them watching her from across that upscale bar five years ago, but he was Italian. He did that to women. It wasn't personal.

But there had been something deeply personal between them for a few hours in his penthouse. She could feel the same magnetic draw he had exerted on her while he'd slept and fought not to shiver under the memory of giving in to that pull, pretending it was a dream to justify losing herself in her long-repressed physical desire for this man.

As if he read the direction of her thoughts, he sharply averted his gaze then brought a cold glare back to rake it down her dress. She knew it to be flawless yet still sensed she was criticized and found wanting.

Was that her own baggage of insecurity or a genuinely harsh judgment on his part? After all, she was a grieving widow. What business did she have wearing something pretty, in snow white of all colors, showing up at his extravagant party?

Wrenching nausea, the kind that had nothing to do with physical illness and everything to do with anguished emotions, clenched in her stomach. She'd had months to sort through it all. She'd owned up to her part in this conception. Paolo only needed to be informed because it was the right thing to do. She hadn't come here looking for love and devotion even if a tiny part of her had hoped…

He held her in contempt, though. She could see it. Like everyone else, he believed Ryan Bradley had been beyond reproach. Everything she did, every action she took, should be an honor to her fallen hero of a husband. What Lauren wanted or needed didn't matter. She certainly shouldn't look at other men. Sleeping with them was a crime worthy of a scarlet A. And if that man happened to be her husband's best friend? Well, that put her somewhere lower than a garden slug.

Which was a judgment she might have accepted if she had been the one incapable of fidelity, but Ryan was the adulterer, not her. That was the other reason she'd allowed herself to make advances on Paolo that night. Her marriage had been over months before Paolo confirmed Ryan's death and made it official.

With a dignity she'd found somewhere between hating herself and feeling grateful to this man for the baby in her womb, she left off touching her hair, clutched her pocketbook to hide her nervous trembling, and said with a hint of challenge, "You look very nice, too. Thank you."

His gaze slammed back to hers, sharp with disbelief at her subtle criticism of his manners.

Holding that hostile stare was hard, but she wasn't as timid as she used to be. At least, she was trying not to be.

A light of reassessment altered his expression and she felt as though the charged air between them ramped up several notches.

With a lift of one brow that seemed to say, *Is that how we're playing?* he offered his arm. "I didn't see your name on the guest list. What a pleasant surprise to have you turn up anyway."

By that she understood she was hideously unwanted here. It was almost enough to make her
run barefoot back to Montreal.

"I'm making a point of doing a lot of things I
barely dreamed of before," she retorted lightly.

Avoiding the flash of warning in his gaze that
asked, *Before what?* she set a tentative hand on an
arm that felt as hard as banded steel.

"Traveling alone, trying new styles..." She would
have gone on, but touching him again made heat
coil through her.

This arm had held her in a dozen ways three
months ago. Protective across her shoulders. Comforting behind her lower back. Soothing when it
tightened across her stomach and drew her into his
spooned strength. Resistant across her chest when
he'd tried to refuse her sexual invitation, then vital
and possessive when he'd draped her thigh over
his forearm, making her his.

Physical need, stronger than any she'd experi-
enced in her life, made her falter, tightening her
hand on his sleeve, leaving her weak and quivering and fighting to hide it. They'd only taken two
steps and she couldn't prevent herself from sway-

ing against him as she fought to regain control of herself.

His arm turned to marble beneath her touch and he glared down at her. Everything in him gathered with rejection, like she was a leper.

"May I?" A man with a camera stepped before them.

Lauren froze in a kind of preternatural fear while Paolo condensed into a statue of impatient tolerance, willing to put up with her closeness out of duty.

Appearances, she thought. Heavens yes, we can't let down appearances.

Rather than smiling at the camera, she lifted her bitter gaze to Paolo's, seeing yet one more person in a sea of them who hid authentic feelings behind a facade. How disappointing to find out he was like all the rest.

Incredulity flickered in his dark brown eyes. And challenge. He didn't like being found wanting. Not at all. As their stare held, heat crept into his gaze, burning with knowledge. Intimate, sexual knowledge. He picked her apart and left her in pieces as the camera flashed, momentarily blinding her to Paolo's final rebuff of all she offered.

"Beautiful," the cameraman murmured, reviewing the camera's screen.

"Grazie," Paolo said dismissively, and drew her away. "Champagne?"

"After I've eaten," she demurred, searching for a private corner where she could get this over with and disappear. Seeing him was far, far harder than she'd expected. He'd been incredibly remote the morning after as the press release was read. She'd been frozen herself, just trying to get through the days until the funeral. The Bradleys had closed ranks, creating a buffer that kept Paolo from approaching. At least, that's what Lauren had thought at the time, when she'd spared a thought beyond her inward twisting of anguish, grief and guilt. She'd been grateful not to speak to Paolo after the shameless way she'd behaved.

Now, however, everything was different. Or was it? She was still dying inside at her brazen behavior. Part of her was second-guessing her decision to come here. She'd been a fool to imagine there'd been any emotion on his side that night. Obviously it had been nothing more than an exercise in physical gratification. He wasn't showing any enthusiasm for seeing her. This was the same man who'd frozen her out most of the times she'd seen him. Best to cut to the chase and leave.

"Actually, I'm not here to wine and dine, Paolo. I need to speak to you. I tried to book an appointment through your assistant."

He kept a bored look on his face while people around them cast curious glances their way. "With the death of your husband, *cara,* I thought my ties to you were finally severed and we'd never speak again." *Nice.* He really did despise her to the core.

Because of Charleston? Or did it go back to her wedding day?

She had never understood Paolo except to liken him to Ryan: driven by his ego and masculine desires, slaying women without even trying because females eagerly set themselves up for the little death such potent men promised.

And delivered. She almost had to shut her eyes to beat back the memory of how beautifully Paolo delivered.

She reminded herself she was one of many women who wished they knew him better, but honestly, she'd had so few occasions to try. He'd bought her a drink in a bar despite being engaged to another woman then sat back while his friend pursued her. He'd kissed her with unexpected passion at her wedding reception then snubbed her when Lauren tried to speak to him a few years later at Ryan's birthday.

In Charleston he'd been solicitous and tender, then ardent and insatiable.

Then cold. Subarctic cold.

She hadn't exactly been impressed with herself at that point, making love to her husband's best friend the night before his death was announced, so she ought to face his hostility without feeling as though a chisel was being hammered directly into her heart, but his enmity hurt. He didn't have to be madly in love with her, but he did owe her a few minutes to tell him they had a tie between them that could never be severed.

A woman in midnight blue chose that moment to join them, forcing Paolo to drag his gaze with visible annoyance from trying to penetrate Lauren's to the inquiring face of a woman with unmistakable Italian coloring.

"Isabella," Paolo said in a tense tone. He slid a possessive arm around her and brushed her cheekbone with his lips, provoking a surprised widening of her eyes. "May I introduce Mrs. Ryan Bradley. An old friend."

His tone was dismissive, emphasizing "old." Former. A possession of his friend.

Isabella was twenty if she was a day, and Lauren felt ancient before her. She was acutely aware of her status as a widow. A cynical and jaded one.

Nevertheless she managed to offer a courteous, "Call me Lauren, please. Since no one else seems to." She cast that at both Paolo and the world, accompanying the request with an offering of her hand.

It trembled. She hadn't let herself think of Paolo with a woman in his life. Seeing him touch Isabella made sharp talons rip into her from the soles of her feet right up to the base of her throat. Of course he had women in his life. They all did.

Isabella cast a look between them, trying to read what may have happened between them during the infamous disappearance of Captain Ryan Bradley's wife into the rarely used penthouse of his close friend Paolo the night before Captain Bradley's death was revealed.

Paolo maintained a stoic expression. *Nothing,* his flat gaze said.

Lauren had perfected the same poker face and baldly showed it to Isabella.

While remaining burningly conscious that her waistline would soon reveal their big fat lie.

"I can only stay a few minutes," Lauren declared, thinking that must sound bizarre considering she'd obviously spent as many hours on her appearance as every other woman here. "Would you be very offended if I claimed a dance? I only wished to say hello to Paolo as I was passing through New York. He's been so kind." She choked a little on the adjective.

Had it been pity that had prompted him to make love to her? The thought had been lashing her like a whip since he'd given in with a shudder and a curse. Her hand longed to go to her waistline in an attempt to protect her developing baby from such a pitiable start.

"Of course," Isabella said magnanimously. "And please accept my sincere condolences."

Appearances again. It seemed Lauren was just as guilty as the rest of the world. Sickly guilty, if she let herself dwell on it, which she tried not to. She woke in a cold sweat too often, worrying her husband's death was her fault. Ryan hadn't been happy about her request for a divorce. Had it made him extra reckless when foiling those terrorists?

Pressing the suspicion to the back of her mind, she accepted the condolences for the sake of Ryan's family, squeezed Isabella's hand with appreciation and avoided the delving look Paolo turned on her. Ten minutes, she swore to herself. Then she could wrestle herself out of this dress and all the other confines of her life. She would be a butterfly emerging from a chrysalis, able to fly into places she'd never dreamed when she'd been a lowly silkworm tied by emotional threads to her grandmother's estate of maple trees.

"Why here, then?" Paolo asked as he steered her toward the dance floor, his tone growling with disapproval. "If you only wanted a few minutes of my time?"

"I—" She had to pull herself together as he set confident hands on her, leading her into a waltz. It had been years since she'd taken the lessons, imagining dancing with Ryan in Vienna when she joined him there, but the trip had never materialized. Nothing truly exciting had ever happened to her.

Except discovering she was pregnant with this man's baby.

Lauren faltered, probing her memory for the steps and searching for a clear thought in the haze that closed in with Paolo's disconcerting presence.

Wide shoulders filled her vision. His clean-shaven jaw tempted her lips to lift and taste. He'd been stubbled and masculine and hot, so unquench-ably, passionately hot. Demanding when he took control. Skilled and confident and ravenous. Like a wild animal let out of his cage, running her to ground and feasting on her.

Her breath shortened and sexual heat suffused her, making her quiver, filling her nostrils with his familiar scent. It had only been the one night. How could she know his dark, espresso scent so well she could find him blindfolded in this heav-ily-perfumed crowd?

"You're making a fool of yourself," he muttered.

The words sliced through her, withering a very sensitive nerve. She knew she lacked experi-ence and sophistication. Why else had her hus-band cheated on her? Paolo didn't need to rub it in, though.

Lauren flashed him a livid glance from eyes that

burned, but he wasn't looking at her. He wasn't aware she was melting under his touch.

"Be a merry widow for your next husband," he said scathingly. "Ryan deserves better."

Ryan had lived a double life.

"He had his mail delivered to his mother's," she said, shying at the last moment from shattering Ryan's precious image. He was dead and he'd died with honor even if he hadn't entirely lived so. "The invitation was forwarded in a packet they sent to me."

It had been postmarked the day Ryan had gone missing. The engraved envelope was one she'd seen annually and always wound up throwing away because her husband had never been home to take her.

"Initially it only meant that you'd be in New York. I wanted an appointment to see you in your office, but your schedule was booked and my grandmother's closet is full of dresses like this. When else would I wear one?"

Pride had made her do this. Pride and a perverse desire to thumb her nose at expectations and propriety. Frances Hammond had come home pregnant with her head held high. Lauren Bradley intended to leave the same way.

She lifted her chin, daring him to take that away from her.

Nothing. Not one iota of reaction. Only a disinterested, "Why did you want to see me?"

The moment of truth. She waited until he'd spun her so her back was to the majority of the crowd, making lip-reading from across the room less likely. "I needed to tell you that I'm…" She found the Italian word she'd looked up especially. *"Incinta."*

If the language switch caused him any confusion, he didn't show it. In fact, he showed little reaction at all, beyond one contemptuous glance down his nose.

"Congratulations. Whose is it?"

CHAPTER TWO

LAUREN HAD PREPARED herself for many reactions: anger, blame, suspicion that she was trying to trap him, even disbelief in the context that this could have happened to a pair of otherwise responsible adults. She had not imagined a denial of any involvement whatsoever.

Behind her burn of outrage raced a trail of humiliation. Did he really imagine she'd taken other lovers besides him and her husband? Well, why not, based on the way she'd made love with him as though she was starved for it? Her throat clogged and mortified pressure built behind her cheeks.

She stumbled out of sync with the music, forcing him to pull her a fraction closer to steady her. He was an iron cage around her, supporting her while trapping her in this farce of a dance.

She moved as though swimming in molasses, a bug caught in sap, soon to be immortalized in amber. Light-headedness combined with the spin of the dance made the room swirl around her while her stomach turned over. Whatever blood had been circulating through her drained into her toes, leaving her chilled to the core.

Somehow she reached through the miasma of shock to locate contempt for a man who dared to denigrate her when he'd been in that bed exactly as long as she had.

"You never struck me as lacking intelligence, Paolo." Her voice was soft yet layered with frost, frigid as a Canadian winter. "You deserved to know, so I told you. Have a nice life."

She pushed away from him, head high, tears thick in her throat.

No, Paolo thought. It was the only sound in ears pulsing with his boiling blood. Ryan's? Another man's? *His?*

No, no, no. He was not stupid enough to fall for that again. His ex had pulled this same trick for a direct line to his fortune, complete with another man's baby conveniently conceived at an appropriate time to make it plausible. He'd unquestioningly done what was right for his child and the payback had been six months of melodrama, scheming and bitterness that kept his heart hard to this day.

He had vowed not to let any woman tear him to pieces again, but as Lauren left him on the dance floor, he felt like an actor who'd been abandoned on stage, the spotlight hot and white upon him, props gone, lines forgotten. He'd felt the same way after their night together, when she'd disappeared into the clutch of grieving Bradleys, leaving him to cope alone.

Despite his exceptional reflexes and honed instincts, he didn't know how to react to something so unexpected and threatening to his carefully structured life. Especially when lust was clouding his vision and frying his mind. Dancing with her had been as erotic as making love to her.

Then it struck him. She hadn't said it was his, only that he deserved to know. Because the *perception* would be that it was his.

A string of violent Italian curses fed through his psyche as he strode after her. To his irritation and disgust, Vittorio stopped her before either of them had wound very far through the crowd.

"I must confess, I didn't recognize you from your photos," Paolo heard as he came upon them. "I'm

Paolo's cousin, Vittorio. I knew your husband. I'm deeply sorry for your loss."

Paolo couldn't stop the territorial slide of his hand beneath the drape of Lauren's silk wrap, fingers splaying over lithe back muscles that stiffened at his touch.

The tumultuous instinct to guard her, *own* her, while his brain reminded him she was the enemy, tangled his thoughts, making him say harshly to Vittorio, "She's leaving."

"So soon?" Vittorio was enjoying himself, aware something was afoot and determined to have a piece of it.

"I only wished to put in a brief appearance," Lauren said with surprising solemnity. "Given this event benefits cardiac research. My grandmother had a heart condition so I wanted to show my support."

The unexpected revelation set Paolo back on his heels. He was instantly sure the records would show a very generous donation next to her name and even though a string of zeros often meant nothing to people in a crowd of this financial rank, the catch in her voice underlined her sincerity. Her devotion to her grandmother had always been something he respected about her.

The phrase *"had a heart condition"* pinged inside his skull. The old woman was gone? He unconsciously gentled his touch, offering a caress of comfort.

Lauren shifted her weight, subtly removing herself from contact with Paolo's fingertips, the only sign she was aware of him, while she continued speaking to Vittorio.

"She passed away earlier this year." She controlled the hitch in her voice. "The loss was overshadowed by other events, but it does make a night like this quite difficult. I hope you'll understand and excuse me?"

"Of course," Vittorio said with a gallant bow before stepping aside.

Paolo slid his arm more securely around Lauren's waist and tightened it, pinning her to his side before she could sweep herself away.

She flung him a look that lashed like a bolt of lightning, gilding him in an exciting sensation of pleasure-pain. It was completely at odds with the fading spirit and demure manner she'd been projecting seconds ago. No one else saw it, but he tasted the slap of challenge and the hot blood it left in the corner of his mouth.

Everything about this woman provoked a visceral reaction in him and Paolo had to temper a grin of exhilaration. If she wanted a fight, she'd come to the right place.

But she was pregnant, he reminded himself, fighting an impulse to grip her with hard, controlling hands the way he would anything that fought his will: a race car, a powerboat, a fighter jet. At the same time, he thought, *Pregnant,* and knew he should lift his red-hot palm right off her.

Despite knowing he should never have touched her in the first place, he kept her from moving with a flex of his superior strength. Whether she was actually naming him the father or warning him of the perception, he was facing a firing squad. Perhaps he owned some of the responsibility for that. He'd brought her into his home and made love to her. It had been foolhardy and wrong, but it had been the first time in five years that other spouses had not stood in the way. In his weakened state, he'd let long-suppressed desire overtake him.

It should have been a bittersweet aberration tucked away and forgotten, but she had decided to bring an infant in a basket to his doorstep. Having the baby turn out to be his was the only way he could forgive her for doing this, but he simply couldn't let himself believe that she was telling the truth. Other motives were too quick to present themselves: his fortune, for starters.

They needed to talk.

"Play host while I escort Mrs. Bradley to her room," Paolo said without looking at Vittorio, perversely pleased with the flush that poured into Lauren's cheeks and the way her burgeoning breasts heaved against the line of her dress.

"That isn't necessary," she said through her teeth.

"*Si, cara,* it is. Very much so."

Lauren refused to speak to him as he accompanied her to the elevator. Part of it was stubborn fury, the rest complete intimidation. She was catwalk height, like her grandmother, five-ten plus more in heels. Somehow Paolo's looming six-three had never penetrated, probably because she'd rarely stood this close to him.

Threat radiated off him. Not physical threat, but the impression that he was on the prowl to crush her in some way and was merciless enough to do a fine job of it.

"So?" he demanded when the elevator doors enclosed them. "Whose is it?"

She dragged her gaze from his magnetic reflection and looked scathingly up at the man himself, mortified to acknowledge that desire still gripped her. It had always been there of course, sublimated, rejected and ignored. That's why she'd so rarely stood near him or held a real conversation with him. That's why, after trying to speak to him at Ryan's thirtieth birthday and receiving nothing but disparagement, she'd told herself she hated him.

She had convinced herself she would never see him again, but three months ago she'd had nowhere else to turn. At best she'd hoped for a civil phone call that might or might not have shed light on Ryan's disappearance.

Twenty-four hours after the pleading message she'd left on his voice mail, however, he had walked into the Bradleys' cold, silent mansion like an avenging angel, eyes only for her. It was the last thing she had expected and inexplicably, despite all the turmoil around her, her inner freeze had thawed into a flood of warmth and relief. Her heart had begun to beat again.

Let me take you out of here, cara. He'd been like a mug of cappuccino, all coffee tones in a fawn leather jacket over dark chocolate pants. His jaw had been sprinkled with a sexy, overnight stubble and his brown eyes had been liquid with empathy and sorrow.

She'd gone with him because she had trusted him. The painfully awkward interactions in the past had fallen away and they'd been two people in the same crisis willing to cling to each other to survive it. She hadn't gone to his penthouse because she was sexually attracted to him. She hadn't wanted—

Well, that wasn't true. She had *always* wanted on some level. Involuntarily.

She dropped her defiant gaze from his, swallowing back embarrassment over the way she hadn't stopped herself reaching for him in the dark.

Forget it, she commanded herself, trying to ignore the clamor in her that said, *I don't want to forget.* It was over. If he'd had a weak moment of desire then it was her good fortune. She had the baby she'd longed for. Every time she thought of the life growing in her, her heart expanded to fill her chest with the sweetest ache. All she was really concerned with now was proceeding with life as a mother.

"It's yours, Paolo," she said in a husky voice aimed at his shoes, then realized she was doing it again, hanging her head as though she had something to be ashamed of. Jerking her chin up, she set her jaw and braced herself against the feeling of teetering like a plate on a stick. "I don't care whether you believe me," she declared.

"Good," he said as the car floated to a halt and the doors opened. "Because I don't."

She choked on offended fury. She cared. Of course she cared. This was their *baby*. All the maternal instincts she'd kept in stasis for years rushed forward to stand up for their child.

"How dare you call me a liar over something so important?" She made no move to exit the elevator.

He put out a hand to hold the doors, his scornful gaze flaying her into sandwich meat. "I've been down this road. How could you think I'd take your word for it?"

She didn't know much about his marriage, only what Ryan had told her: that his ex-wife had plotted with her lover to con Paolo into child-support payments. The plan had backfired when he had insisted on marriage. He had unraveled the subterfuge right before Lauren's own wedding to Ryan and the marks of being taken advantage of had been carved into his brutally handsome features while he'd stood next to Ryan at the altar. Ryan later admitted that just before the ceremony, Paolo had tried to talk Ryan out of marrying her.

Then, grim and cynical, Paolo had barely been civil at the wedding reception, leaving a strong impression he blamed Lauren for timing the event to happen as his own marriage dissolved.

She didn't own a crystal ball. She couldn't have known. She had felt awful and tried to apologize. Now, frozen in the elevator, she unwillingly relived how he'd told her to leave him alone and she hadn't listened, reaching out instead to try to comfort him. He had brushed her off, started to turn away, then had spun back and pulled her into him like a lifeline.

He had opened her right up for the passionate kiss he'd drawn from her with seductive ease. She'd forgotten everything, most especially that she was newly married. Nothing had come back to her until Paolo had drawn back to murmur something against her lips and Ryan's voice had interrupted at the same time. Then Paolo's gaze had turned cold and vindictive. Women were fickle and treacherous and easy, he'd implied with a rake of his gaze down her wedding gown as she had moved to her husband's side.

After behaving like that, she should have seen that he would lump her in with the woman who'd turned him into such a cynic about female honesty. Lauren put out a hand to steady herself against the cold mirror, biting back a protest that she was different. She had no way to prove it though. Not when she'd been the one to initiate the lovemaking in Charleston.

How obtuse was she that she hadn't seen this coming? But she'd known she was above women who played foul so it had never occurred to her he'd accuse her of such a thing. Lauren had never been a flirt, or a strategist, or a manipulator. Paolo saw her through his tainted glasses, however, and it made her feel dirty.

Why did she care, though? She'd been prepared to raise this baby alone from the moment she had suspected she was pregnant. She had come to New

York convinced she didn't need or want his support on any level.

While a hidden part of her had basked in the chance to draw a little of Paolo's attention one more time.

Even though his regard had always scared her a little. Like a possum under a suddenly bright light, she'd always skittered away or curled into herself or into the nearest shadow—preferably those cast by larger-than-life people like Ryan. But she had thought, right up until Paolo's first caustic remark tonight, and especially after his tenderness in Charleston, that he'd felt at least a little warmth toward her.

His expression held nothing but cynicism and contempt, however, as he waited for her to absorb his rejection of her claim.

She hid her devastation behind a proud posture, keeping her back arrow-straight as she finally preceded him from the elevator, faltering when she realized this wasn't her floor but a private suite. "What—"

"We need to talk," he said, stabbing security buttons beside the elevator panel. "In private, and uninterrupted."

"Are you out of your mind? Dragging me to your room is what started this!" Despite her apprehension, an irrepressible jolt of anticipation hit low in her belly. The unwanted receptiveness to his advances made her feel intensely vulnerable. For another long second, she couldn't move, couldn't look at him.

"Throwing Charleston in my face right now is a mistake, I assure you," he said dangerously. "How far along are you?"

She set a tender hand on her waist, breathless with alarm. She was locked in a situation she should have been smart enough to avoid while sensual memories wouldn't shake from her scattered mind. And she felt weak. It occurred to her how badly she had neglected this baby today, too preoccupied with facing Paolo to take care of herself and the growing life inside her.

"You can do the math," she murmured.

"Three months since we were together, but I can see the weight gain starting. Is that why you slept with me? To disguise some married man's bastard?"

"Oh, stop it!" she spat. "Have I asked you to *be* a father?" After losing her own and suffering Gerald as a substitute, she'd concluded that father figures were overrated. Her grandmother had filled all the necessary parental roles just fine, thanks.

Wanting to finish with him before her delicate hold over her control slipped completely, she paced into the lounge, bypassing the narrow aisle between the sofa and coffee table for the wider band of area behind the furniture. As she spun, her skirt billowed in a way her lungs couldn't. She was aware of his scrutiny like a scientist behind a mirrored wall, watching a distressed animal seek escape from its cage.

"Yes, people are going to notice soon that I'm pregnant," she stated, trying to drag deeper breaths into her compressed lungs. "They're going to speculate that it's yours. I owed it to you to prepare you for that, so here I am."

"So you're keeping it." The words were flat and uninflected.

It was an unexpected blow that winded her.

"Of course I'm keeping it! I've waited years for a baby." She tried to say it calmly, but she couldn't help the residual fury over Ryan's duplicity, letting *her* try to explain to his mother why they weren't conceiving when he had privately known exactly why. "How can you suggest I not keep it? You're Catholic. And don't you dare ask if I slept with you to get pregnant. I'll slap you, I swear I will. I thought I was infertile."

She spun again, still pacing, feeling like one of those little metal ducks quacking her way along the upper ledge of a carnival tent. Paolo's laser gaze seemed to track her like the red dot of a sniper's rifle while he weighed her words.

"I know this baby looks like a disaster, but it's a miracle." Her agitation at having to explain without being able to *explain* kept her blood vessels tight, her muscles tense, her focus dim and narrow on the walls rushing by.

"I'm willing to minimize the damage by leaving the country, but it's going to come out, Paolo." She'd managed to ignore her anxiety over that eventuality, but it threatened to overwhelm her as she spoke of it. Her feet moved quicker and she felt the walls closing in. Her mother's shame and disappointment, Ryan's mother's horrified incomprehension… It would be a nightmare and Lauren didn't even have her grandmother to stand by her.

What she wanted, what she'd come here for, was rescue, she realized. Deep down, she had hoped for the same help and support he'd offered in Charleston.

She wasn't going to get it though. She really was alone in this.

Eyes stinging at how inexorable it all was, Lauren made herself halt, growing aware that she was gasping breaths in, but was forgetting to let them out. A clammy sweat condensed on her skin and her vision faded to white. She was hyperventilating and even though she tried to make herself stop, panic at not tasting any oxygen stole her self-control, making her try harder to catch her breath.

Paolo said her name in a sharp tone. She blindly looked to where she thought he was, but she couldn't see him. Her hearing was muffled as though her ears were filling with water. She moved her lips, trying to tell him, trying...

Paolo had never seen anyone crumple like that and it stopped his heart. Somehow he kept her from hitting the floor, catching her in his arms while his knees took the brunt of the marble beneath the thin rug. Gathering up miles of silken fabric with a slender, limp shape inside, he pushed to his feet, heart pounding with dread as he deposited her on the sofa.

Her color was ghastly. All he could think was that she was miscarrying when she'd just called her baby a miracle. He had an inkling of how devastating that sort of loss could be and couldn't stomach it happening to her.

Razor wire coiled in his chest, squeezing mercilessly as he fumbled his mobile from his pocket and tried with trembling hands to locate the number of the pediatric heart specialist sipping champagne in the Grand Ballroom.

Lauren's lashes fluttered before he found it. Her dazed eyes blinked open and something warm and lovely shone up at him before confusion clouded in. She automatically tried to sit up, but fell back quickly. Her breaths sounded like anxious gasps, frightening him.

"I can't breathe." She reached for her back. "Open my dress."

"What?" *Dio!* He could kill her he was so terrified. Clattering his mobile onto the coffee table he rolled her into the sofa back and used both hands to release the tiny hook-and-eye closures down her back. There were a million of them and his fingers were big and clumsy. "I was trying to call a doctor. Are you in pain?"

"No, I—"

He overrode her with a string of curses as the panels of her dress peeled open to reveal a silken cord tied punishingly across her pale back. As he hurried to release the strings, he exposed a pattern of thin welts criss-crossing her satiny skin. "What in hell! The laces have nearly cut through to your ribs."

"It's not that bad, is it? It doesn't hurt." She ran light fingers over the indents while her rib cage expanded and her body relaxed into softer lines. "I'm fine," she dismissed on a long, easy sigh. "It was just a little tight."

"A little?" Appalled, he traced each mark, ensuring they were superficial enough to fade.

Her spine made a subtle arch under his touch. Goose bumps rose across her flexing shoulder blades. Her reaction was so immediate and honest it sent a sexual zing through him, enticing him to slow his stroking into a deliberate caress. He recalled that her skin tasted exactly as smooth and creamy as it looked. The desire to bend and press kisses to her neck and shoulder until she moaned with need nearly overtook him.

He forced himself to stand so he couldn't touch her, mind reeling at how close a call that was. His body was shaking and his blood sizzling. "Why would you wear something so dangerous?" he charged.

"Dangerous?" she repeated with a gurgle of humor. She rolled onto her back, hugging the loose front of the dress to breasts that remained invitingly plump against the amethyst edging. "Since when are gowns deadly?"

Her smile invited him to join her in laughing at absurdity. Part of him wanted to let it happen. When she forgot to be shy, she was quite animated and fun.

And sensual. Her eyes grew languorous as she gazed up at him. Her color was flowing back in a warm glow.

"Shoes are regular serial killers, but dresses are harmless," she teased.

He couldn't help the twitch of humor at the corner of his mouth. "I've seen dresses short enough to take a man down. Whiplash is a common occurrence."

Her smile grew. "I nearly died of embarrassment in a bathing suit once. True story."

"I would say nothing is safe, but that's probably riskiest of all."

He'd taken it too far, his voice lowering to an intimate tone as he pictured her naked. The irrepressible attraction between them rose like a ring of spitting fire, urging him to move closer to her. It took everything in him not to lower onto her and do exactly what he'd done the last time he'd been alone with her. They'd been completely naked, nothing between them, nothing.

And it had been so *wrong*.

He curled his hands into fists, refusing to let himself absorb the implications. "This isn't funny, Lauren. None of this is the least bit funny."

Her mouth flinched in startled hurt at his return to recrimination. She threw her arm over her eyes to block him out and started to say, "I know, I'm s—" but flattened her lips to stop herself. "I was nervous, so I didn't eat. That's why I fainted."

"That was stupid!" His alarm for her climbed into the rafters. "I'll order something. Are you on a special diet?" He was across the room with the hotel phone in his hand before her plea stopped him.

"Paolo, don't. Not here. Not like this." She lowered her arm to reveal a disturbingly unguarded expression and nodded at her state of undress. She wasn't taking this as lightly as she seemed. "Just pour me a glass of soda. Something with sugar, but no caffeine. And maybe a banana or one of those oranges? Then I'll go back to my room and have a proper meal sent up."

He fetched what she'd asked for, assembling her micro-meal on the coffee table then standing by as she carefully sat up.

The intensity of his tension struck him. He watched her pour and sip with a silent will for her to consume faster, like this was anti-venom she was taking in and her survival vitally important to him. The reality was, they were acquaintances through her husband. He didn't know her well at all and couldn't afford to trust her no matter how attracted to him she acted or how vulnerable she seemed.

From day one she had thrown out those conflicting signals, seeming interested yet always turning to Ryan. She wasn't the first woman to feed her ego by using one man's attention to make another jealous, but she was the only one who had managed to both draw Paolo in and incite his green monster. Paolo refused to be treated as a plaything. It made him all the more certain she was setting him up in some way.

"You need to get back to your party," she murmured, carrying the icy glass of soda to her temple.

"No one will miss me," he countered, even though he was distantly aware of the same thing.

"Isabella will," she admonished. Then, keeping her face averted, asked, "Are you going to marry her?"

He hesitated. This news of Lauren's was more than even his lightning mind could process quickly, but he couldn't turn his life upside down without thinking it through. It would be humiliating to believe her and discover he'd been tricked again. Best to stay the course until he had better evidence for a correction.

"It would be a good match," he said, hammering Isabella's top qualities for both their benefits. "Her father is at the UN, her mother works with an international aid organization. Isabella understands life on the stage of global politics. Yes, I intend to marry her."

Lauren made a noise of acknowledgment that almost sounded like the gasp from an absorbed blow.

Her reaction inexplicably caused invisible wires to pull him tighter than his tension already had him. A pike of misgiving speared through him and he instinctively wanted to rethink everything he'd just said.

It was exactly the turmoil he wouldn't allow her to put him through. He brushed aside the detour into self-doubt as she spoke again.

"I didn't hear anything about love. That was the problem with your first marriage, wasn't it?" She kept her attention on the orange she was separating into sections, holding it well away from her gown.

He stared at the top of her head, willing her to look up at him and dare to say that. At the same time, his gut twisted with guilt. It was true, he'd had very little affection for his ex, but she'd still managed to devastate him. It was one reason he was determined to pin his future on Isabella and not a woman he truly loved. To be betrayed was one thing, to love and be betrayed would be impossible to bear.

"Love is for fools," he muttered.

With a snort of cynicism, Lauren chortled, "Ain't that the truth."

Hearing her echo the sentiment irritated him. The way she had turned to him in Charleston had proved to him she wasn't as devoted to Ryan as she'd portrayed through her marriage. This was further evidence she had scorned a man who had worshipped her.

"I guess that makes Ryan a fool, marrying for love," Paolo said scathingly.

"Are you serious?" Her amber gaze flashed up like a splash of bourbon, stinging with hot-cold. "If he loved me so much, why did he spend all his time on the other side of the world taking insane chances with his life? He married me because I was raised to wait until I had a ring on my finger and he wanted bragging rights."

"A clever ploy on your part, seeing as his family is quite well off," he shot back, while a flash of Ryan's smug victor's grin hit him square between the eyes. There could be some truth to her claim. He had another suspicion about his friend's motives, one that was even less complimentary. They had always been competitive with each other, he and Ryan. It was usually good-natured, but there were times it had been cutthroat and Ryan had been in no doubt that Paolo found Lauren attractive.

No doubt.

"It wasn't a ploy, it's the truth," Lauren bit out defensively, pulling Paolo's thoughts from a dark place he rarely visited.

It was a place of bitterness he barely understood because he never examined it, but it filled him with enough acrimony to challenge, "You married for sex then?"

Disbelief dropped her jaw before her outrage fell away to wounded pride.

Her stunned silence pricked his conscience. He almost began forming an apology for crossing a line, but a self-conscious flush flooded into her cheeks. She looked naked and culpable, but her expression carried an edge of defiance that gave him a tingle of premonition. He unconsciously braced himself.

With her blush firmly in place, but a disconcertingly frank look sweeping over her, she sat straighter and said defiantly, "Perhaps I did marry for sex. I was curious and not confident enough to believe any other man would be interested, but I did love Ryan, in my immature way."

That was too much honesty. He looked away, wanting to refute what she was saying by pointing out *he* had been interested, but that would only muddy already dark waters. Immature he would accept, while the rest he held in reserve. He needed to view her as deceitful to keep his distance. Otherwise he'd have to believe everything she was saying about this baby she was carrying and where would that leave him? Not upholding the honor of his family name the way he'd sworn to do after so disgracing it with his ugly divorce.

He would have to believe that when Lauren had woken him from the first sleep he'd had in forty-eight hours by sliding her caressing hand into his shirt, it had been from genuine desire, not ulterior motives.

The pulse of desire that hit with that possibility was a sledgehammer straight into his gut, bathing him in heat. His hungry gaze moved restlessly to eat up the way her shorn head revealed her slender neck and the graceful slant of her nude shoulders. Her deshabille gave off a sexy, yet ingenuous appearance.

Don't fall for it, he cautioned himself, but couldn't help thinking that no matter whose baby grew in her belly, she was still a woman without a husband to provide for her. She was susceptible and he was, at his core, a protective man.

He was duty-bound to protect his family, though. And what did it matter whether she had married for love or not? She was also admitting to resentment that her husband had been away a lot. What she'd done during those long absences was very much up for scrutiny. Perhaps he should take her at her word that she wasn't asking him to be a father, only wanted to warn him about an impending media storm.

"Where are you planning to go?" he asked, hitching the knees of his pants as he sank into the sofa opposite her.

"I told you. To my room." She darted out her tongue to catch the juice from the orange that ran down her finger.

She might as well have stroked that tongue where he'd feel it most. His loins were still pooled with simmering heat and he reacted as though she had licked him, the strain turning into an erection so swiftly, he stifled a grunt of pain. If he could have stood, he would have walked out on her.

"You said you were leaving the country," he reminded in a hostile clip that caused the brightness in her gaze to dim. Good. There was no room for sensuous picnics between them.

"Italy," she replied stiffly.

He choked, certain he'd misheard. "Like hell you are. That's my home."

"I'm sorry, do you own the entire country? The brochures didn't say." That sexy mouth had a quick motor behind it, didn't it?

"Did I misunderstand what you said about minimizing damage? Or do you only intend to be discreet where it affects your interests?" he asked.

"It's not like I'm going to call up your family and introduce myself! I want to look up my own, if you must know."

He leaned back, stretching his arms across the sofa so he wouldn't lean forward and throttle her. A ferocious sensation accosted him each time he came back to her assertion that the baby was his, like poking an abscessed tooth with his tongue. He dismissed it, focusing on the more immediate problem.

"This is the first I've heard that you have Italian relatives. Who are they? Where do they live?"

"My mother's father was Italian, not that she'd admit it." She broke off a piece of banana and carefully nibbled. "My grandmother came home pregnant. Mom was her love child."

Lauren's lashes flickered as her gaze dropped and her brows tugged together. He heard her thoughts. Her baby wasn't a love child. What was it then? A mistake? The product of a one-night stand? *His?*

The questions carved an ever-deepening hollow behind his breastbone, one that he pitilessly ignored.

"The man who would be my grandfather was married," she continued. "His wife was very sick. They had a daughter and he didn't feel he could leave either of them. That's what he told Mamie. I don't know if it was the truth, but Mamie loved him." A smile of wistful affection quirked her lips. "Until the last day of her life."

"Odd that you didn't inherit her sense of loyalty, given how much she meant to you." It was a nasty thing to say, but he didn't like how easily she was drawing him into her poignant little web.

She took the insult with a tiny sniff of hurt, then opened guileless eyes and responded, "My Italian blood must have led me astray."

He ground his teeth. "You have no concept what kind of lion you're riling, do you, *cara?* I may wear bankers' suits, but I know how to scrap."

She paled a bit as she carefully wiped her fingers on the cloth napkin he'd provided, but she didn't intimidate. Her gaze was level when she met his.

"Honestly, Paolo? There's only one thing you could do to truly hurt me. That would be to take this baby away from me. I don't think you'd harm either of us and it doesn't sound like you want to fight me for it, either. You'd have to admit it's yours, and you hate me too much to do that." Her lips went bloodless as she pronounced that. Her eyelashes flickered as though she didn't quite understand how that could be.

While he caustically wondered how she imagined it could be otherwise.

For five years she'd been tossing shimmering ropes of curiosity at him even as she attached herself to Ryan. When he'd met her, he'd been days away from his own marriage, but unable to let the wolves prowling the bar they'd been in to consume her. He'd pulled her and her cousin into his booth while he waited for Ryan, entranced by Lauren's shy, understated wit and killer legs. When Ryan had arrived, Paolo had expected his friend to remove with her cousin to Ryan's hotel room, but no. His friend had turned his good-ol'-boy charm on Lauren and she had blushed under the attention of two men.

Engaged, there was nothing Paolo could do but warn his friend against being cavalier with an obvious virgin. He'd been shocked six months later when Ryan had announced he was marrying her, partly because Paolo hadn't realized they'd kept in touch. By then he'd been so deeply entrenched in the loss of his father and minimizing the damage of his marriage imploding, he'd convinced himself that whatever attraction he'd felt toward Lauren had been a bachelor's last hurrah.

Then he'd glimpsed her arriving at the church and the magnetism had been even stronger than he'd remembered. Unbalanced by it, he'd blurted out a hasty are-you-sure lecture to Ryan that had gone nowhere. Inexplicably, Paolo had been filled with rage as the vows were spoken. The entire ceremony had become a living hell, his abominable desire for Lauren growing like a snowball careening down a hill. He'd tried to drink it away, unable to make sense of his reaction while longing for the evening to be over.

Then Lauren had followed him outside, looking like the most delectable innocent ever sacrificed to a man's basest hunger. *Ryan's* hunger. Paolo had kissed her. The hard, passionate kiss they'd shared burned on his lips and conscience to this day.

If she hadn't returned his ardor all of this would be different, but she'd kissed him as though he was the only man she would ever want, and that had made everything worse. He hated her for letting the kiss go on too long, for escalating behavior he'd put down to intoxication and grief into something unforgettable. He inwardly cringed from the weakness it represented and the hurt he—they— had caused people he cared about.

The degradation never left him. *Best* man. To this day, no one else had asked him to hold the position, always joking it wasn't in the groom's interest. Of course he hated her for that. Charleston was merely fuel to the fire while this fiasco with a baby made it impossible for him to feel anything toward her but animosity and suspicion.

"Your silence says everything, doesn't it?" she said with a little quaver in her voice. "That's fine. As I said, the baby is my only vulnerability so unless you decide it's yours, you're completely powerless to touch me." Setting aside her napkin with a hand that shook, she secured her dress with crossed arms and stood to turn her back. "Could you close the hooks so I can go to my room?"

He didn't move, eyeing that slender back where the punishing marks were fading. Her shoulders seemed to have fallen a notch and that made something teeter in his chest before he quickly closed off to anything like mercy or regret. *Focus.*

Nevertheless, he tasted a hint of self-contempt that he had it in him to be cruel to a woman, even one who wasn't as defenseless as she looked, but he had a lot to safeguard.

"My family is in government, *cara,*" he reminded gently. "I'm hardly powerless. I'd hate for you to endure a long flight only to be turned away by customs."

She spun slowly, her spine stretching as she lengthened it with umbrage. "You wouldn't."

Try me, he dared with an unflinching gaze, feeling a catch of the old, reckless Paolo who had gambled too often in too many ways. It filled him with elation.

"Be a good girl and go back to Quebec," he cajoled, adding a smile of condescension for good measure.

Her nostrils flared as she drew in a breath like a cloud gathering volume. Her fists closed into angry knots of white against her bare, upper chest as she kept her dress pinned to her front.

"Don't you dare," she said from between clenched teeth, "tell me to rattle around that empty mansion again. That's all I've done for months and I'm sick of it!"

Her quiet ferocity should have warned him off, but it stoked his inward excitement, priming him for a badly needed contest of wills.

"I'll do what I please," he stated with quiet brutality.

"So will I! Ryan was supposed to send for me after Mamie died and instead—" She stopped herself. Her gaze averted as her face crumpled into anguished struggle to overcome unvoiced, but very intense pain.

Ryan had disappeared.

Paolo's desire to punish her evaporated in a

wrench of grief and self-disgust. Her pain *hurt* him. If she broke down, he didn't know what he'd do. He couldn't hold her, couldn't touch her. He knew that way led to madness.

"Lauren," was all he could say. He leaned forward, unable to help that her name came out like an entreaty. *Don't fall apart. Don't make me bed you again.*

She took his murmur of her name as an attempt to persuade.

"No," she refused truculently. "I won't do it, Paolo. I spent all those years with Mamie because I wanted to and I don't feel like I gave up my youth the way everyone said I would, but I do recognize that I have only this tiny window between now and when the baby will tie me down. This is *my* time and I'm taking it. Don't try to stop me by having me questioned at the airport. You won't like what I tell them."

Her harsh threat, so surprisingly effective, chilled him to the bone. He couldn't take it lightly. "You're bitchier than you look," he muttered with unmitigated contempt.

Lauren jerked as though that verbal slap had landed well, but tossed her head to shake it off.

"I don't want to do it. It's up to you. I didn't come here to start a war. I've told you, I don't want anything from you. I'll try to keep the secret as long as I can. Despite—"

Her voice caught and she hugged herself tighter, swaying a little.

He glanced at the plate and calculated she'd had two sections of orange and a bite of banana, chased by a little soda. Damned fool. He stood, prepared to catch her again.

"Despite the circumstances under which this baby was conceived, I'm happy about it," she rushed to say.

What circumstances were those? his most cynical side longed to demand. Better that than dwelling on a memory so bittersweet he couldn't let it out of its vault. He had to keep his attention on not taking her claim at face value. Paternity could be established in time but the reality of today was, no matter who had fathered her baby, once the pregnancy became evident, the world would look to him as the culprit.

And until he knew indisputably that it was his, he didn't intend to be accused of it.

"My dress?" she prompted, turning her back again.

"How will you get out of it once you're alone?" He slipped off his tuxedo jacket and dropped it across her shoulders, swamping her narrow back and making her look younger and more innocent than he could stand.

"There's nothing I can say or do to keep you from going to Italy?" he demanded.

"I leave tomorrow. It's a done deal."

"Cosi sia," he muttered. *So be it.* At least she'd be out of the States, the country that would be most scandalized by a pregnancy that spoke of a betrayal against their national hero.

Taking her elbow, he steered her toward the elevator. She was tense in his grip, her weight leaning into his hold more than he expected and she was very pale. The evening had taken a toll. Perhaps the baby had, as well. An unwanted clench of concern firmed his grip on her arm.

At the same time, his mind raced. He had intended to be in the air first thing with Isabella, Vittorio and Vittorio's parents, delivering Isabella to her parents' immediately upon arrival. All his Christmas arrangements would have to be reviewed and reconsidered. His entire calendar for the next quarter, perhaps the next year. Perhaps his entire life. *Damn you, Lauren.*

"You're landing in Rome?" he questioned gruffly.

She paused to glance up warily as they stepped into the elevator. "Milan. Why?" she challenged with suspicion.

"Milan," he repeated under his breath, thinking it was both more and less convenient. His agile mind leapt to possibilities.

Thankfully, they saw no one on the way to her room. He took her keycard and opened her door while she shrugged out of his jacket and returned it. When she lifted a strained look to him, he saw only pouted, tender lips, and a melancholy shadow in her eyes. And yet the sensuality was there, the child-goddess yet to be awakened to her full potential. Those conflicting signals of innocence and sin fascinated him. He wanted to kiss her.

"You left Charleston so abruptly after the funeral. I never said—"

His heart clenched. "Don't thank me, Lauren. I won't like it," he warned. And yet... *No.* He tamped down hard on feelings he never should have had, never should have given in to.

"Goodbye," she finished with gravity. "I never said goodbye."

The finality in her tone and the resolve in her expression grabbed him by the throat.

"Ciao," he managed past the strangling fist. He was clinging to hostile suspicion and inescapable guilt like it was a life raft, trying to convince himself this *would* be goodbye if he could only prove the baby wasn't his.

But he couldn't say it. Not yet.

"Buona notte, bella."

CHAPTER THREE

LAUREN DIDN'T SLEEP well. Paolo's husky voice kept snapping her awake as he spoke her name in that sexy inflection of his, murmuring his throw-away endearments. He wasn't beside her when she woke though, making the bed feel too expansive and empty.

She was such a fool. She'd slept alone more than she had alongside her husband, yet after one night with Paolo she now woke so lonely she wanted to die. What a dope.

She caught a few winks on the plane. International first class was a lot more comfortable than flying small-town air to see her mother in Manitoba or flying in a military aircraft to meet Ryan at his parents' in Charleston. Funny that she'd flown dozens of times, but had never gone farther than a few states or provinces over.

The realization gave her pause as she waited for her luggage to arrive on the carousel. She was really here, in another country, being bold and in-dependent. Her grandmother hadn't been able to travel—or do much of anything, which is why Lauren had moved in with her at eighteen; Ryan had invariably wanted to visit Charleston when he had leave. The closest she'd ever come to striking out for adventure had been when her cousin, who was going to school in New York, had begged her to visit.

Lauren's heart panged with pity for her timid, nineteen-year-old self. She hadn't wanted to go, but her grandmother had made her. Lauren had been the worst shrinking violet in those days, trembling in her cousin Crystal's skintight cocktail dress, dreading someone would peek past the loose hair she was hiding behind and discover she was un-derage. *Upscale bars are where you find rich hus-bands,* Crystal had said, insisting they go on the stroll for one. When the tall, dark, insanely hand-some Paolo had approached, Lauren had been cer-tain he was the owner coming to kick her out.

He'd offered to buy them a glass of wine.

Lauren had been stunned by his melted-chocolate eyes and her first experience of being being hit on, even in an offhand way.

Her entire being had become electrified by his admiring gaze. Incinerating with embarrassment, she had peeled her gauche stare from this dazzling man to look at Crystal—who'd accepted the invitation with élan. Gorgeous, wealthy men hit on her all the time.

He was engaged, Paolo had confessed. *But that doesn't stop a man from enjoying pretty company while he waits for a friend.* His friend had been Ryan.

Ryan hadn't made her stammer and writhe with self-consciousness so she'd focused on him and tried to ignore that all her inner workings were fixated on the compelling man sitting so close to her.

Lauren sighed, wondering whether her life would have been different if she had said no to Paolo's glass of wine. Or no to Crystal's insistence that she come to New York.

Or yes to Paolo at the wedding reception. An image flashed in her mind of the way Paolo's hair had fallen over his tortured brow when Ryan had come upon them in the garden, Paolo's invitation to leave with him still hanging in the sultry air. Paolo's resentful glare when Lauren had moved to her groom's side to ease the animal tension radiating off both men, still chilled her.

She had thought the men might come to blows, but Paolo had been looking for a fight and Ryan had known it. He'd said so later.

She could still taste the tang of whiskey that had flavored Paolo's tongue and had known his pass toward her had only been a drunken, impulsive act. He had made the overture yet she'd always sensed he blamed her for it. His anger still stuck and stung.

Ryan hadn't blamed her, though. That probably should have been an indication that he wasn't exactly invested in her fidelity. Instead, it had been three years before she started to get inklings he wasn't the most faithful husband.

Did Paolo blame her for that kiss? Is that why he'd cut her in two at Ryan's thirtieth, pithily dismissing her worries that her husband was fooling around? He'd made her feel so foolish for her suspicions, but if she'd gone on her instincts, she wouldn't have still been married to Ryan when he was killed. She wouldn't have the memory of Paolo's gaunt, shattered look when he'd broken his terrible news that Ryan was dead.

She could live without all those other painful memories, but as anguished as her night with him in Charleston had started, she couldn't regret it. Even in light of his hostility last night, and the likelihood that he'd only been using her in Charleston to curb his grief, she was grateful and happy they'd made love.

He wasn't.

She had replayed last night in her head until she'd been ready to drink herself into oblivion, letting each inflection and livid glance score her again and again. He hated her for making him betray Ryan, and no wonder. As early as that first time she'd met the two of them, she'd seen a truly remarkable friendship, one born when they'd been children attending international schools where Ryan had been an army brat and Paolo the son of an investment banker.

On the surface it had all been playful one-upmanship. They'd competed for grades and saved each other's lives countless times while risking their own in foolhardy cliff dives and motorbike races, but she could see there had been a foundation of unequivocal trust between them. Ryan might have forgiven Paolo for his moment of weakness at their wedding, accepting Paolo's word that he was drunk and upset about his own marriage falling apart, believing Paolo's vow that it would never happen again, but Paolo would never forgive himself.

Last night, Lauren had almost told Paolo that Ryan had cheated on her, but she knew from the one time she'd suggested it that Paolo wouldn't believe her. And what kind of person spoke ill of the dead, especially to his best friend? Nevertheless, she couldn't help thinking that Paolo might take a different view of their transgression in Charleston if he understood. She hated knowing he hated her.

But she hadn't taken the chance to set the record straight and now she'd never see him again.

That realization, studiously avoided through the long night, suddenly impacted her strained, over-tired emotions with blunt force, filling her with a swell of pain very much like grief. Hot tears gathered in her eyes and she dropped her face into her hands, edging toward a breakdown in an airport full of strangers a million miles from anything familiar.

"Signora?" A concerned male voice pulled her face from her hands.

As she jerked her head up, she saw her luggage go by. She reflexively stepped forward, trying to grab it before it went around again. The man, a conservative middle-aged Italian in a nondescript suit, retrieved it for her.

It was such an unexpectedly gallant thing to do it yanked her out of her maudlin self-pity and put a fresh smile on her face. He insisted on helping her all the way out the doors of the airport. By then she'd learned he was only in Milan for the day on business, returning to his family in New York for Christmas.

"Oh, *signore*," she said as he guided her toward the curb. "The hired limos seem to be that direction—"

"*Grazie,* Bruno." Paolo came around from the driver's side of a virile black sports car. His eyes were hidden behind aviator glasses despite the drizzling sky.

Lauren's insides took flight and her mouth went dry with shock.

Paolo stole her bag off her cart and stowed it where she thought the engine ought to be. Her new friend slid her other small bags alongside it and slammed the lid as Paolo opened the passenger door.

"Rapidamente, per favore," Paolo prompted her. "I'm parked illegally."

"But how—?" What was he doing here? She began to tremble, struck by shock and the irrepressible excitement she had thought she'd never feel again. It was so invigorating!

An official blew a sharp whistle and shouted something.

"I have your luggage," Paolo reminded, pointing to the seat where he wanted her.

"That's extortion," she argued, but regressed into her compliant old self and ducked into the car, glancing back to thank Bruno. Paolo shut the door in her face.

She couldn't make sense of this turn of events. Despite her pride in traveling alone, she was enormously relieved. She wanted to hug Paolo and had to restrain herself as he slid behind the wheel and zipped away from the curb, pressing her into her seat.

"Buckle up," he ordered.

"How did you know I was—" *Bruno.* She looked for the man as she reached for her belt, but he was gone. "How did you know that man's name?" she demanded, putting two and two together and coming up with fraud.

"He's my head of security." Paolo settled himself with a lift of his long back and a rock of his wide shoulders. One confident hand remained on the wheel as he tuned the radio from news to classical, switched gears, adjusted the rearview mirror, and zigzagged through traffic, passing sedans and shuttle buses. "I put him on your flight last night."

On my tail, you mean. She would have said it, but brake lights glowed—

"Watch out!"

Paolo made a lightning move to nip around the stalled car.

"Would you quit driving like a maniac? You're going to kill us both." Adrenaline stung her arteries. She blamed the dangerous roads, but suspected it had more to do with the dangerous man next to her.

"I'm trying to get us out of this traffic. Just because you don't know how to drive in America." He grew serious, geared up and down and jockeyed for advantage among his equally reckless compatriots.

"I'm Canadian, and we drive like there's ice on the roads because there often is." Still, Lauren couldn't help choking on a giggle as she observed the craziness of it all, looking for the landmarks she'd seen from the air. "I am definitely not in Kansas anymore."

"I thought you were living in Quebec?"

"I am. Was. Paolo, *how?*" She opened her palms in bafflement, wishing away the skip that plucked at her heart when she looked at him. But he was so masculine and sure. His sunglasses obscured his eyes, setting off his blade-straight nose, his stern jaw, his mouth with its narrow upper lip and the squared-off but full bottom one.

That mouth had traveled everywhere on her, tender and wicked and determined to draw forth every last ounce of pleasure. Her stomach contracted in a clench of desire remembering the way he'd devoted himself to kissing the arch of her foot, the backs of her knees, her inner thighs....

Flushing, burning in a hell of sins, she jerked her gaze back to streets she didn't see. "You didn't say anything about coming to Italy last night," she said in a strained voice. "Your assistant said you were leaving town after the benefit and gone until the New Year, but she didn't say where you were going. How are you here ahead of me? Were you on my flight, too?"

"No, I arrived ahead of you." He pursed his lips with dismay before saying, "I didn't wish anyone to know we were associating beyond our brief conversation last night. You have put me in a difficult position. You understand that, *si?*"

She had put *him...?* Defensive anger poured through her. She'd grown up with step-siblings who had always pointed to her as being at fault and she didn't take that sort of blame any longer.

"I didn't rape you and steal your sperm, Paolo."

"Who knows you are pregnant?" he demanded.

"Just my doctor."

"Who else?"

"No one! All the books said to wait three months before telling anyone."

"They don't mean the father, Lauren. Or did you try telling him and things didn't work out? Is that why you've come to me? What happened with the real father? Tell me. I'll help you."

Lauren stopped thumbing the clasp on her pocketbook, annoyance making her heart ring and come out fighting. "The real father didn't believe me and is behaving like an ass."

He shot her a sharp glance until he read her meaning in the withering look she offered. His sexy mouth firmed into a hard line.

"You *are* being an ass," she asserted. "I needed time to figure out what my life would look like as a single mother so I kept it to myself. Why didn't you call?" she challenged. "You knew we hadn't used any condoms."

A muscle twitched under his eye. "I believed you were unable to get pregnant so even though I didn't mean to take that risk, the likelihood of conception didn't seem high enough to follow up on."

All she heard was the first part and it caused her a sensation like a knife had been thrust into her throat. Another one turned slowly about eight inches lower, deeper in her chest. "Ryan told you I couldn't get pregnant?" she choked out.

"Not in so many words, but I'm Italian. We have big families. You always struck me as—" He stopped, seeming to rethink what he'd been about to say.

"What?" she prompted. Sad? Pathetic? Gullible? She braced herself, willing him to continue.

"You seemed like a woman who wanted to be a mother," he allowed as though it grated to acknowledge that. "Whenever I saw Ryan, I naturally asked if babies were on the way and he always said, 'No luck yet.' So I knew you were trying."

"Very enlightened of you to assume it was my deficiency, not his," she bit out.

"No matter whose deficiency it was, you have to admit it's a stretch for me to believe one night is all it took for you to get pregnant after that many years of trying with your husband."

"Well, you haven't had a vasectomy, have you?" she blurted.

The car jostled slightly as he reacted, sending her a sharp look. "What are you saying? Ryan wouldn't have done that."

Any remorse she felt over revealing her husband's duplicitous nature was quickly overshadowed by her tremendous bitterness over the secret he had kept from her. The many secrets.

"He did exactly that," she said, scraping the words from the bottom of her trusting heart. "Before we married. And never told me."

"Then what makes you believe he did it? Why

would he even consider it before having children?"
he argued.

"I don't know." She scowled, still capable of a
shred of empathy for the man who'd had an even
worse relationship with his father than she had
with her mother, times a million. "You know how
difficult his father was," she charged begrudgingly.
"I can't help thinking that had something to do
with it."

Paolo shook his head, unable to comprehend this
piece of information. He wanted to dismiss it completely, but when he glanced from the road ahead,
he saw Lauren struggling with myriad emotions,
fighting to hold on to her pride. Her bottom lip
trembled with injured dignity before she firmed it,
causing a strange tremor to hit deep in his chest.

This baby is a miracle.

He pulled his attention back to the road, uncomfortable with what she was saying because it sup-
ported a profile of Ryan that Paolo had long been
trying to put from his mind. He grew even more
uncomfortable in front of Lauren, given a certain
conversation they'd almost had at Ryan's birthday
a couple years ago.

"Are you sure, Lauren?" he blurted, willing her

to be mistaken. "How did you find out if he didn't tell you?"

"Their family doctor came to see Elenore a few days after the funeral. She was a wreck and I said that I wished we'd at least been able to give her grandchildren and he said, 'Well, I tried to talk Ryan out of that vasectomy, but he insisted.' He said it like he thought I knew. I pretended I did while I finished my coffee, then I went upstairs, packed my things and flew home to Quebec."

Lauren was still ashamed of that abrupt departure, but she'd hit the end of her rope in playing the mourning widow. She had already been months into accepting Ryan's philandering, but it had been a fresh blow to count up all those years of anguish at what she had believed was *her* inability to conceive. She was just grateful Ryan had apparently used protection against disease while he'd been sleeping around because she had tested clean.

Tell him, she thought, glancing at Paolo. Tell him that Ryan was probably also ensuring none of his many affairs turned up with the sort of complication Paolo was currently facing.

She couldn't do it, though. Paolo's face was a wall of stubborn refutation, not unlike the way he'd looked the other time she'd brought up Ryan's peccadilloes. Paolo didn't want to hear anything against his friend and she wasn't in the mood to be called a liar.

Deflated by his stubbornness and the long flight, she asked, "How far to my hotel?"

"You're not going to a hotel. I told you, you've put me in a difficult position. The last thing I'll allow you to do is run around Milan attracting attention."

"Like whose?" she exclaimed. "I'm not even traveling under my married name. I'm back to being Lauren Green, complete nobody."

"Don't be naive, *cara*. After the stir you created last night, our photos are everywhere, all tagged to raise the same speculations as three months ago. Your new hair is a red flag. The paparazzi would love to spot you, especially going into a doctor's clinic. Did you have plans to do such a thing?"

"Such a scandalous thing as having my blood pressure checked? Yes, I made arrangements. It's a sensible precaution. But what stir? I was at your party for ten minutes and hardly spoke to anyone."

"Exactly. Everyone was asking about the mystery woman who stole the host." He muttered a few base curses in Italian. "Even Isabella was fielding questions. It was very awkward."

"Well, I'm sorry for Isabella," Lauren said sarcastically. "Maybe for your fiancée's sake, the next time you have a one-night stand, call after a few weeks to see if there's anything you need to know."

Dead silence, then a dangerous, "Did you really just say that to me?"

"Is my naïveté showing? Because the not calling is what makes it a one-night stand, is that right? I'll work on getting that right while I'm here."

"That's not funny, *cara,*" he said in a gentle voice that chilled with warning.

"I'm not trying to be funny. I'm trying to get over the fact that you don't want anything to do with me, yet you're abducting me. Why? Just take me to my hotel," she insisted. "Or I will use my very decent Italian and my new mobile phone."

She was so enamored with the cute little gadget, she couldn't resist pulling it from her pocketbook to show it off. "Look, it even has the two-way camera and global coverage. That means I can do this." Holding the locked screen before her as though she had a connection, she spoke in Italian. "Good afternoon, Officer. I am being held against my will by this man." She turned the phone to Paolo's supercilious expression.

Before she realized he could move so fast, the phone was in his breast pocket and his hand was draped casually over the stick shift again.

"Hey!"

"Take a nap," he said. "We have a long drive ahead of us."

It was the same condescending trivialization of her needs and feelings she'd grown up with. She automatically swung through the old gamut of anger draining into the helpless sadness of feeling like she could never win, would never matter, couldn't do what she wanted and would only be chastised if she did.

She looked out the side window, catching a glimpse of a charming bell tower overlooking a square of some kind. Chocolate shops? Perfumeries? What else did the square hold? She wanted to know and she was old enough, and free enough, to make a decision like that for herself.

"People always wondered why I chose to live with a sick old lady and that sort of dismissal is why. All I ever heard growing up was, 'Do as you're told, Lauren. Don't fuss. It doesn't matter whose fault it was, just say you're sorry and don't talk of it again.' Even Ryan did it to me. 'Do we have to talk about that now? I'm only home for three days.'"

With a burst of pent-up frustration, she flung her head around to say, "I'm sorry my organs are perfectly healthy and I dared to get pregnant when you were only taking pity on a weeping widow. It won't happen again, trust me."

Assaulted by a fierce need to self-protect after that outburst, she struggled to do the zip on her jacket, then folded her arms and turned her back on him as much as the tight confines of the bucket seat would allow.

He reached to make an adjustment on the console and heat poured onto her feet. "Ryan never told me you had this kind of temper." He sounded amused which made her want to hit him, but she kept her face averted, so overwhelmed by everything that had happened in the past twenty-four hours, she could have cried.

"Like Ryan ever got to know me, home for three days out of a hundred," she grumbled.

"Lauren," he said with an imploring tone that nearly got to her.

"Oh, just forget it, Paolo. I want to enjoy the scenery. Drive to Sweden if you like." She waited a beat then goaded, "I'll rent a car when we get there and go wherever the hell I want."

Women.

Paolo had thought Isabella's stilted kiss-off when they had landed had been bad. *My father texted. He thinks, under the circumstances, it's best we don't see each other.*

Paolo was edging toward being a pariah again. One favor three months ago, one good deed for the sake of a valued friendship, and his life was coming undone at the seams again.

Letting out a measured breath, Paolo eyed the woman beside him, wondering how he'd let it unfold this way. After he'd swept up the pieces of his broken marriage and shattered reputation, he'd been so careful, so very careful to keep himself in line. He struggled every day against reckless impulses and had learned to double think his gut-level decisions with coolheaded logic. Brick by brick, he'd rebuilt himself and the family bank into something that was solid and trustworthy. With the economy as shaky as it was, he couldn't afford any missteps.

And yet he'd stumbled right into Mrs. Bradley. *Ryan has disappeared, Paolo. No one will tell me anything. Please help me.*

For some reason he still had her message on his voice mail. He couldn't bear to listen to it, but couldn't make himself erase it.

Paolo wasn't a man who believed in extrasensory perception, but he'd known Ryan was gone the second he'd heard her strained voice. As boys, the two of them had nearly killed each other dozens of times, but no matter how far Ryan might have fallen or how long it took him to come out of the water, Paolo had always known Ryan was still alive and right behind him.

He frowned, thinking about that: *right behind him.* They'd first met while sharing classes at an international school outside Singapore. Initially, they'd been too competitive to like each other. Paolo was used to outpacing other students without even trying, but suddenly every quiz or spelling bee or sport match was a contest with the American boy. Ryan had been determined to overtake him in every arena.

In later years, Paolo would learn that the Bradley family motto was "Good, better, best. Never let it rest. Do your good better. Do your better best." And if you didn't, you caught hell when you got home.

Paolo had his own motto: Lead. You couldn't do that from second position.

The turning point had been a cross-country race at semester's end. They were twelve and well out in front of the rest of the pack despite the rain and mud and steep climb through slippery jungle. Paolo had just splashed through a swollen creek, Ryan was hot on his heels, when a sound—

To this day Paolo didn't know what self-preservation instinct had made him turn and grab his competitor and drag him forward. A sound, something in the way the muddy water slid fast under his feet...primal awareness? Whatever it was, it saved Ryan from a slough of earth that scarred the hillside with a deep gouge. They had both stared at the gaping gorge where they'd both had their feet seconds before.

"We have to stop the others," Paolo had said.

Ryan ran ahead to the finish line in record time.

Paolo waved the next boy off and sent him back to stop the other runners. Later, they were touted as heroes—something that seemed to become an ingrained piece of Ryan's makeup. He had found a way to earn his father's approval. He had embraced putting his life on the line for others with future acts of derring-do.

That identity had followed Ryan into his career in the military. He'd been determined to save the world. He'd mocked Paolo mercilessly for being destined to take up banking of all professions, rather than high-octane black ops. Paolo had quelled his envy of Ryan's action-packed life by doubling down in his studies, covering the bases for his eventual career, but pursuing a dream at the same time. A dream he'd had to abandon into a sensitive scar that Ryan never failed to poke.

Through all of that, somehow both men had overlooked the true danger in what Ryan did.

Paolo had had to face it when Lauren had reached out to him, however. Even though, deep inside, he'd sensed he wouldn't hear good news, he'd made calls. He knew people, influential people. He'd quickly learned what was being smothered by a government trying to salvage a mission gone terribly wrong.

Paolo had been struck by survivor's guilt. Was it really duty that had led him to take up the family profession? Good sense? Or plain old cowardice? Why was it Ryan's responsibility to take the narrow chances in the name of peace and freedom, and not his?

If he had been with his friend, could he have saved him?

Somehow he'd found himself on a plane, the knowledge of Ryan's death a secret that ate like a cancer inside him. He'd had to tell Lauren. Had to see her. He hadn't questioned that compulsion, had just followed it. Some things couldn't be said over an electronic connection, he supposed.

Ryan's family had been there when he'd told her. It couldn't be avoided. They'd had a right to know and they were as devastated as expected. The Bradley mansion had become the pit of hell and Paolo hadn't been able to bear it, not when his own emotions were hanging by a thread. He'd needed to leave that place and there was Lauren, looking so alone, her hands like icicles when he picked them up, stiff and frozen. He hadn't examined his decision to take her with him. He hadn't even given her a choice; he'd just pulled her away.

Alone with her in his suite, he'd been able to let down his guard. It hadn't been long before they'd been crying in each other's arms, eventually moving to the bed out of physical and emotional exhaustion. He had spooned her warmth into the hollow of his body as comfort for both of them. That was all it had been intended to be.

Then he'd woken more aroused than he'd ever been in his life, his skin tight and hot, his need to thrust into her primeval. He wished he could say he had put up a fight, but it had been the most pathetic of his life. He'd pressed her away from kissing his throat, but all she'd had to say was *Paolo.*

His name. She'd known it was him. That was all that had been important in that darkened room. His heart had pounded hard, trying to fill the palm stroking his bare chest. Having anything between them at that point had become intolerable.

If it had been just the once, it might have been forgivable, but they'd kept going, orgasm after orgasm. He'd stripped her naked, kissed and licked every inch of her, not letting himself think of anything but owning her in every possible way.

She'd been a greedy sensualist, deliciously unin-
hibited, biting his shoulder, legs like a vise around
him, so wet and tight and insatiable he'd almost
died.

Perhaps he should quit wondering how she could
be pregnant and consider how she could *not* be.

He glanced at her, thankful her back was to him
and she couldn't see he was sweating and having
trouble controlling his breathing. Desire drummed
like an inexorable march inside him: want, want,
want.

All he had to do to kill it, however, was remember the self-loathing that had filled him when he'd
woken with her naked body entwined with his,
her hair spilled like a dark stain over his chest and
stomach. She'd been equally appalled, sitting up,
moving away. Silent. Neither of them had said a
word, only departed for separate showers.

What kind of people behaved so dishonorably?
Paolo hated both of them, himself for regressing
into the man who succumbed to the desire of a moment, Lauren for not stopping him. She possessed
the power to make him disregard consequences
and seize something he never should have touched
in the first place. It infuriated him. She made him

edge toward being the irresponsible man he used to be and he couldn't have it.

He glanced at her again, suspecting by the way her head lolled and her arms had loosened that she was fast asleep. So much for scenery gazing.

Completely misplaced protectiveness moved in him. She would be the instrument of another downfall if he didn't handle this with absolute care and clear thinking.

Dio! The woman had a tongue, though, and the things she said provoked the most elemental reactions in him—emotional, difficult-to-temper reactions.

He couldn't allow it. *Rent a car and go wherever she wanted.* Like hell she would. She could have her Italian holiday if she insisted, but not under his mother's nose. Not a chance.

CHAPTER FOUR

PAOLO'S WARM FINGERS stroked the side of her face in a tender caress. Lauren sleepily turned her lips into the skin at the inside of his wrist.

He jerked his touch away and a curt profanity hit her ears.

Lauren blinked her eyes open, disoriented and aghast by her instinctive nuzzling. She'd known it was Paolo, so why…?

Hot with mortification, she looked down to find herself fully dressed in the passenger seat of his car. Beside her, he was turning away to make room for her to exit, leaving the door open. A crisp wind swirled around her, eager to sweep the cobwebs from her mind.

"Where are we?" she managed to stammer as she swung her feet to the ground.

She was dizzy from his touch so she stayed sitting, taking in the sculpted landscape of winter-stunted grass and bare shrubs. In the middle of the well-kept grounds a charming stone house rose in peaceful, old-world charm, its rock walls twined with dried vines. Wrought iron balconies jutted out here and there and behind it, across the valley, blue sky and snowcapped mountains formed a backdrop.

Curious, Lauren stood and the intensely blue lake, marbled with restless licks of white, opened below her, stretching an expansive arm into a stunning view that magnanimously stated *Welcome.*

"Oh," she sighed in awe. Wrapping her fingers over the top of the car door, she drew in the crisp, clean wind and wondrous serenity. Alongside the house, stone steps led down to a glittering turquoise swimming pool that steamed on a terrace halfway to the beach. Cushioned loungers sat invitingly next to it, angled toward the view.

"You'll enjoy your stay here, then?"

Lauren hitched her elbow over the car door and regarded him. He stood in profile to her, facing the water, fists in his pockets. He was so compelling yet remote. His wall of aloof detachment held her off, giving her a sense of irrelevance. She had the impression she was something he wanted filed away and forgotten.

Balming lips that felt dry and nerveless, she questioned, "Stay?"

"I've arranged this villa for your use while you're here."

So arrogantly conscientious. It would be funny if it weren't so annoying. And indicative of his great desire to make her disappear.

Ignoring a pinch of childish insecurity, she shut the car door and moved to the top of the steps. "That's very generous of you, Paolo, but if I'd wanted to stay in a villa miles from civilization, I would have arranged for it myself. I could, you know," she told him with a boastful glance. "My grandmother made a fortune in real estate. My step-siblings think that's why I moved in with her, to secure an inheritance. I didn't, but she left everything to me anyway." She couldn't help grinning at that. Mamie was the only one who'd treated her decently and Lauren revered her for it.

"Then there's Ryan's share of his mother's wealth," she added, laying it on as thick as the moss on the stones beside her, determined to make him see she wasn't without resources.

"It galls Chris no end that I'm keeping my share of Ryan's trust, which is probably the reason I'm doing it since I don't need it. And of course the U.S. government sends me widow benefits." She wrinkled her nose, not feeling as good about taking that money. "If I thought it would go to anything but guns and tanks, I'd refuse it. Instead, I'm rolling it into a program that helps service families who've lost members in the line of duty."

She swung her gaze back to the villa and its charming amenities. "So you see, I don't need you to arrange another empty house for me. But I'll stretch my legs while we're here, before you give me back my phone so I can make other arrangements..."

Lauren's voice faded as she descended the stairs in a lighthearted trip that stuttered Paolo's breath.

"They could be slippery! Slow down. Hold the rail."

"Yes, Mama," she called back, continuing at a pace that made him hurry to be close enough to catch her if she stumbled.

"You're determined to test my patience, aren't you?" he said as they came out on the lawn below. The way she had pressed her face into his hand like a cat seeking more petting was still unsettling him. Now this sass and snub of the trouble he'd taken to accommodate her presence in his country. It was too much.

And was that pose of sexy absorption deliberate? She took in the short beach of rocky sand overseen by a handful of bare fruit trees. He took in skinny jeans that showcased graceful, filly legs. Short ankle boots added length so his eyes couldn't help but travel up and down and up. His palms burned to stroke her slender limbs and test the back pockets that looked so tight he doubted he could slide so much as a single fingertip in, but he very much wanted to try.

The breeze off the water was stiff enough to make her turn up the collar on her smart leather jacket.

"What do you want me to say, Paolo? Wait, let me guess. *Yes, Paolo. Of course, Paolo. Anything you say, Paolo.*" She snorted disparagingly. "Been there, done that, except his name was Ryan. I'll tell you what I'll do, though." She turned to him with a gamine look that encouraged him to believe she could be reasonable. "If I decide to stay in Italy, I'll let you buy this villa for me. It looks like a lovely place to raise a child."

"Stay?!" It was the moment between controlling

the wave-skimming hydrofoil and feeling the deck lift into the zone where you knew you could lose it. He advanced on her, ready to bend her to his will. "What are you trying to do to me, Lauren?"

She took a wary step back, ankle wobbling as she met soft sand rather than firm, dry grass. "I'm not doing anything to you. I'm trying to do for myself, live my life. People like you and Ryan who never answer to anyone don't understand—"

"I answer to everyone!" he broke in with frayed temper. "Do you think the investors in a bank want the head of it caught up in a paternity scandal? *Again?* It's expensive and distracting and when he's there because he cheated with his best friend's wife they question his ethics!"

She blinked in shock, but he carried on, spelling it out for her because she obviously needed to hear it.

"It's a *family* business, Lauren. My sisters and cousins do not appreciate when my fast and loose behavior messes with their living. I know because they've told me. And do you think my *mother,* who already attached herself to one unborn grandchild only to have it snatched away, will appreciate another incident just like it?"

The old helpless, hopeless ache spread shoulder to shoulder behind his rib cage, threatening to choke his voice. He ground words past it.

"My ex-wife's lies broke her heart. I won't let it happen again. So whatever you're doing with your life, recognize it impacts mine!"

His passionate fury was as quick and sharp a slap as the wind gusting off the whitecaps. Lauren worked her heels into the sand so she felt a little more steady, but her ears ached with cold and strain, hearing more than Paolo had said.

His mother wasn't the only one who had become attached to an unborn child.

She hadn't seen past his bitter fury the day of her wedding when he'd been fresh from a fight with his ex. His mood had been an unpredictable storm building quietly on the horizon and she'd thought it was anger at being lied to. He'd been sarcastic and disparaging and portraying himself as inured to sentiments like love. He'd drunk too much and kissed the bride too passionately. They'd all dismissed it as an act of acrimony toward marriage.

It had never occurred to her that his heart had broken the same day his marriage had. He had been grief-stricken, feeling as though he'd lost the unborn child that had turned out to be another man's. Of course he wouldn't let himself believe her when she claimed he'd fathered this one. Of course he wouldn't.

Lauren struggled her heels free of the sand and took a few steps toward the water, tortured by the memory of how quickly she had dismissed Paolo's behavior at the wedding. *He's drunk, Ryan. It doesn't mean anything.* She hated having her own deep hurts trivialized and yet she'd been guilty of doing it to Paolo. Was she coming at their current situation only from her own side and failing to look at how it impacted him?

If she was, she knew why. She didn't want anyone to know how much Paolo attracted her, least of all him. Every deflective action she took was a big, dirty, smokescreen to hide her fascination with a man who was far beyond her league and never likely to return her interest.

Lauren twisted a ring on her finger, not her wedding band, Paolo noted, and was annoyed with himself for attaching significance to that detail. He ought to be concentrating on the chasm of anguish she was churning up: that excruciating time when his father had just died and the baby he'd expected was gone. The spans on either side of his life had snapped and he'd been at loose ends, tumbling disoriented into a bleak gorge, aware there would be a very hard, painful landing before anything would straighten out again.

He'd been wrong to look to Lauren, a freshly minted bride, to soften his impact. He certainly shouldn't be thinking *Grazie, Dio,* because Lauren Bradley was not wearing her husband's ring now.

Her anxious gaze lifted from the water. "I'm not trying to make waves or to hurt your mother or ruin your career, Paolo. But try to understand. I've been patient all my life, waiting to grow up and leave home, waiting until Mamie didn't need me, waiting to join my husband overseas, waiting to see all the places Mamie spoke about. Now you're asking me to wait again? Until when? Twenty years from now when this baby is grown?"

"How is visiting all the places your grandmother talked about living *your* life? It sounds as though you're trying to relive hers."

It was a throwaway comment, something to ward off feeling guilty or softening with empathy, but her face froze. Her surprise faded into stunned culpability as her gaze dropped to the ground. She folded her arms protectively across her chest.

"I suppose that's fair. I didn't see it that way, but…" She moved to the water's edge where she stood in silence for a long time.

After a few moments he ambled forward to join her, sensing he'd shaken her up more than he'd intended to. The weight of defeat in her profile gave him a pang of conscience. He hadn't meant to be hard on her. He knew that a girl in her twenties was more apt to party than nurse an old woman. He couldn't argue that she'd been tied down a long time.

"I lack imagination," she said, rubbing her arms and looking down to kick at the loose stones among the sand. "I always choose the safe route. I told myself I was finally doing something bold and exciting, but you're right. This is just a rerun of Mamie's adventure. How is being exciting so easy for everyone else and I'm just…not?"

That's not true. The statement formed on his tongue, but he swallowed it back, not willing to articulate that even though she usually did her best to look as mousy and timid as possible, she'd been drawing his notice for years. When she laughed, everyone turned to enjoy the sound.

"Define 'exciting,'" he muttered to deflect from what he was thinking. "For most it's a problem with impulse control. A lack of stopping sense. Addiction to adrenaline."

"Is that what it is for you?" Her shiny-penny eyes lifted to his with a light of genuine curiosity and he felt the catch. Immediately the urge took him to hook his arm across her back, pull her into him and to hell with consequences.

He tempered it, pushed his hands in his pockets and stared out across the water. "I suppose it's been all of them at one time or another, but these days it's none," he answered, feeling as restless as the kicked-up peaks on the water. "I'm dull as old knives and intend to stay that way."

She laughed, richly and openly. "Oh, I am so sure, Paolo! Men like you don't change. Life is one big game that you have to win."

"I'm not like that anymore," he insisted, ruffled by her pronouncement.

"No? You don't even have to win an argument?" she teased.

He let her know with a dismissive blink that he wasn't biting on that less-than-subtle catch-22.

She grinned and kicked around the beach for a minute, bending to pick up a stone before saying, "Maybe I'm going through a belated teenaged rebellion. I mostly came to Italy so I wouldn't buckle to my mother's nagging and move back to Manitoba."

In a desultory throw, she flicked a flat stone across the choppy water. It bounced twice on the uneven surface and sank.

"Mothers like their children nearby. That's normal." He found a flat stone and sent it spinning. Four bounces. A warm-up on rough water, but a terrible performance nonetheless.

"She wants me to sit in a chair and not move. She's so high-strung." Lauren sighed with fatalism, thumb working circles on another flat rock. "I try to understand how hard it was for her to be the only one in that conservative rural school who was illegitimate, her mother an exuberant, colorful *hussy*. But honestly? All I can think is how lucky she was to have a mother that was interesting."

She sent her rock across the water. Five. Respectable. For a girl.

"So you feel you have some wild streak that's been suppressed all your life and it's time to let it out? That's fine, *cara,* but not in my backyard." His next rock made six ticks before it struck a wave, preventing it from going farther. He frowned.

"Yes, you've completely lost your competitive edge, haven't you," she said with a knowing smirk that she chinned toward the water. "I'm actually quite good at this. My record is sixteen on a flat pond. What's yours?"

He stopped looking for a good rock. "I can't remember. It's been years since I've done this." He pushed his hands into his pockets so he wouldn't throw rocks until he'd surpassed twenty. It would eat him alive now she'd given him a number to beat. He silently cursed her.

She held out her hand. "Phone, please."

"Lauren—"

"You win, Paolo. I won't flaunt my loose morals all over Milan. I just want to use the map thingy to find a place to eat. You can drop me at a café and I'll figure things out from there."

That didn't sound like a win. It sounded like he wouldn't know where she was.

"Don't be silly. The house is fully stocked. At

least come inside for a look. I'll make you something if you're hungry." He glanced at his watch, recalling that he had a cocktail party at his aunt's tonight, but he had time.

Since he didn't have to collect Isabella, he recalled with a scowl.

"Fine," Lauren said with a short sigh of frustration as she began climbing the steps that led to the pool, planting her feet with little stomps. "But I want it on record that I hate acting like such a doormat."

"Accepting my invitation to cook for you is polite, not weak," he stated.

"You weren't serious, so that makes me weak. The minute someone with the least bit of assertiveness tells me what to do, I fold like a cheap lawn chair. 'Lauren,'" she mocked, "'you have to come to New York. No one else can afford it.'" She swung around at the top of the stairs, tapping her own chest. "I didn't want to go, you know. I didn't want to meet some military flyboy who saw me as a challenge. I certainly didn't want to marry him. If I don't start standing up for myself, I'm going to raise another wimp who trembles like a Chihuahua all her life like I do."

He stood on the step one down from the top, trapped in the stairwell by her passionate speech. She was almost eye level with him and he couldn't get past her without touching her. She had no idea the power she had over him right now. All he could think was that he only had to lean forward a few inches to kiss her. He was the one in danger of trembling and folding.

He kept his one hand locked on the cold rail and flattened the other on the damp stone wall, focusing instead on all that she'd said. Most specifically, *I didn't want to marry him.* He'd been tortured by the vasectomy remark the whole way here, trying to dismiss it, but she'd sounded so bitter and convinced.

"You're shivering like a toy poodle right now," he noted to distract himself from his disturbing inner conflicts. "Go inside. The lock is coded to your birthday."

That made her take a step back. "How do you know my birth date?"

"We met on your birthday."

She snorted. "Crystal lied. It wasn't my birthday. I'm October, not April."

Well, didn't he feel a fool. He'd been using that date as one of his pin codes for years.

The warmth that greeted Lauren as she entered was like a welcoming hug. It wasn't just the central heat, but the open plan and soft lines in the overstuffed furnishings. Even the kitchen with its shiny appliances was a sunny place that encouraged lingering.

"The house is a hundred years old, but the interior was redone last year. Take off your shoes. The tiles are warm," Paolo said.

She did, sighing as she moved through the rooms of heritage blue and sea foam green with splashes of sunset yellow and moody indigo. Upstairs in the master bedroom, translucent curtains framed the windows while French doors led to a private balcony overlooking the lake. The house was roomy yet cozy, extravagant, yet practical. She felt at home.

Damn you, Paolo.

Returning to the kitchen, she found him with his sleeves rolled back, water set to boil on the stove as he chopped fragrant herbs on a cutting board.

"You *were* serious," she said, utterly taken aback.

"Of course."

"Huh. I've been doing the cooking for so long I can't remember what it's like to watch." She looked out all the windows, fingers trailing the smooth edges of windowsills and cupboard doors, eating up quaint details in the decor so she wouldn't gawk at the handsome man moving with such confident economy around the spacious kitchen.

"Why didn't you want to marry him?" Paolo asked behind her, startling her with the question that nudged like a hard shove.

She glanced back, mentally taking a photo of his masculine grace as he skimmed the herbs off the cutting board into a saucepan, filling the room with scents of crushed garlic and tangy basil.

"That was hindsight talking," she clarified, turning back to the window. "Five years of realizing I'd married the wrong kind of man. If I wasted my youth on anything, it was waiting for my husband to come home and start our life together. He was never going to."

"Because he was a military man."

She felt her shoulders fall. More doormat behavior, coming up.

"I don't want to talk about this, Paolo. You'll call me a liar, and the lie is acting like Ryan was a flawless hero who deserved my devotion and still does. I can't keep doing it. I'm too angry with him. It's another reason I had to get away. People kept offering me sympathy and I'm ready to spit venom. It's not nice."

"Because he wasn't honest about not wanting children."

Her chest swelled with unspoken anger. "He wasn't honest about anything," she said, trying to keep her voice even and failing miserably.

Silence.

She curled her fingers in the white lace curtain, trying to hold the guilty anguish at bay, but it pressed outward, making her shoulders ache and her throat sting.

"I asked him for a divorce," she choked out, unable to hold it back. "He didn't want to give it to me. I keep thinking he was distracted and that's what got him killed."

CHAPTER FIVE

PAOLO HAD NEARLY blown off his fingers at eleven, playing with fireworks. This felt like that same moment of realizing he was too close, a life-changing explosion imminent.

Lauren wore the same shattered look she'd had on her face when he had arrived at the Bradleys'. Her skin was nearly translucent, her eyes like bruises. The tiniest flicker of dimming hope quested in her gaze. *Please tell me it's not true.*

An instinctive need to cradle and comfort her had him taking a step toward her before he stopped himself. Was he insane? She had just admitted to being at fault for Ryan's death!

With a distracted glance around, he got his bearings, remembered he was cooking, but at least he was at a point where he could let things simmer since his concentration was shot. He pushed a heavy hand through his hair.

"Why?" he demanded. "Why would you do that

to him? Because he wasn't coming home often enough? You knew what you were marrying."

"Did I, Paolo? Did I really?" She turned all the way around, blinking wet eyes as she fought for control, arms protectively crossed over her chest.

"He was serving his country," he insisted, hammering the points he'd used to justify to himself why Ryan deserved this woman. "Was it so hard to step outside yourself and see there are bigger things than playing house?"

"I wasn't playing!" She came a few steps toward him, angry energy spinning around her like a funnel cloud.

He felt it try to yank him into a fight and rooted his feet, holding his stance against her whirling temper as he searched for the source, sensing it was both in and outside himself.

"I realize you and Ryan got drunk off your faces at his thirtieth," she continued heatedly, "but it was still early in the evening when I asked you if he cheated on me while he was away. You acted like I was the lowest form of life for even thinking it. 'Stop looking for excuses to go after other men,'" she repeated hotly. "That's what you said to me. I felt exactly the way you wanted me to feel. Disloyal, paranoid and wrong. Well, *guess what,* Paolo?"

Her jagged question, laced with bitter irony, made him shake his head, refusing to accept that she knew, that he would be caught out in a weak moment when a prevarication had seemed the lesser of two evils.

He remembered everything about the evening she was talking about: the unwelcome excitement he'd fought as he'd anticipated seeing her; the way he'd struggled not to reveal his resurgence of fascination and desire from the second he'd spotted her; the blaze of heat that had engulfed him when she'd approached him. Even the shower of culpability that had hit him before she'd spoken hadn't been cold enough to kill his desire for another man's wife.

He'd reminded himself that he'd vowed to Ryan that nothing would ever happen again. He'd fought everything he was feeling, telling himself she was being so earnestly bashful and tentative to tease him. She had wrung her timorous hands while her twenty-two-year-old body had been rocking a sexy black cocktail dress and a pair of four-inch heels that had set every man in the room alight.

She was trying to get a rise out of him, to see if she could taunt him into another rash act like at the wedding, he'd told himself. All he'd wanted was to keep a wall firmly between them. There couldn't be any openings, even if he did know something that might make her available....

Paolo had shut down the thought and the conversation as swiftly and ruthlessly as possible. He wanted to do the same now, but Lauren was still talking.

"His lover found me online. I'll be nice and call her that since she believed he truly loved her. That's why she had an affair with a married man, she said. You know what's wrong with digital communication? You can't burn it. Hitting Delete doesn't feel as permanent, especially when every word is imprinted right here." Lauren tapped the middle of her forehead. "No matter how I try to forget, the begging for forgiveness is carved into my psyche. *I knew he was a player but I thought I was different.* Did you know, Paolo? Did you know *then,* when I asked you?"

Lie, he told himself, but he couldn't. Not again. It had chewed on his conscience all this time, but he hadn't been willing to break up his best friend's marriage. Not when he'd nearly done it once before. He had owed Ryan for that and, now he looked back on it, realized it was the reason he hadn't made much effort to see his friend since. He'd resented withholding his suspicions from Lauren. It had made him feel sordid and had severely damaged the respect he'd had for Ryan.

His hesitation was all the answer she needed. Her face paled into a look of disillusionment and betrayal then cold criticism. She took a step back as though repelled, forcing him to rush with a defense.

"I didn't *know*. It was a collection of things I'd heard. A possibility, not a certainty." An awareness that Ryan had never gone long without sex and a remark from Vittorio that he'd seen a man who looked like Ryan in a low-end bar in Berlin, a buxom *fräulein* in his lap.

"Yet you made me feel like a criminal." Her face contorted with the stunned pain of misplaced trust. She bit her lips together, but her chin crinkled and her brows came together in deep hurt.

He knew he had to say something, but couldn't form a reply to save his life, and she was shaking her head, shutting him out, making him desperate. Making his stomach tie up.

With a pained sob, Lauren took off out of the room, snatching up his keys along the way.

"No! Lauren—!" Before he could go after her, a hissing sound behind him warned of a pot overboiling. In two steps he was back at the stove, snapping off the gas then racing after Lauren.

She wasn't tearing out of the drive in his Lamborghini as he'd feared. It was worse. She'd popped the lid into the storage compartment and was trying to lift her bags out of it.

"What are you doing?" He brushed her out of the way to lift them himself. "What do you need so damned badly you'd give yourself a miscarriage over it?"

"Just go, okay? I'll stay alone in your wretched house hosting pity parties for myself the way I've been doing for months and you can go live your life of righteous double standards." She wiped angry fingers under her wet eyes before yanking up the handle of her bag, bouncing and rattling its wheels over the stones toward the front door.

Over her shoulder, she continued acridly, "Go sleep with your future wife and conveniently forget to mention you have a baby on the way with another woman. I'm glad you don't believe me. I hate all of you, the way you stick together and act like your sexual needs are more important than our hearts. No, you're not invited in."

She barred the door when he tried to come in. Pointing to the stoop, she only let him set down her remaining bags then dragged them inside to thump into a pile around her ankles.

"Let me carry them up the stairs for you," he cajoled.

"I'll manage." Standing in the crack of the door so only half of her was visible, she let him glimpse the hollow point in one smudged copper eye. She was devastated, but what was worse was the flatness. Until this moment, he'd always seen a certain reliance and confidence in her eyes when she looked at him. As though she knew she could count on him. Now there was only dejection and betrayal.

"The keys are with the car. Goodbye, Paolo. This time I mean it."

She closed the door and he heard the electronic lock hum into place.

He lifted his finger to hover it over the keypad,

determined to go inside and explain—What? How could he defend himself, or Ryan for that matter? His ex-wife had lied to him. He knew what betrayal felt like. It didn't just undermine your belief in everything you'd been raised to see as inviolable, it crushed your ego. At least he had heard it from his spouse.

He pinched the bridge of his nose, hating himself.

Walk away, part of him urged. *Let it go. Let* her *go.*

Why in hell had Ryan done it? No man in his right mind would cheat on her. She was...

He rubbed the back of his neck, refusing to let himself dwell on exquisite memories of lips supple as rose petals, nipples so turgid and aroused he could hardly stop sucking on them, a wet pocket of heat so sensitive she'd climaxed the first time he'd pressed his finger inside her.

Breathing hard, he made himself return to the car when everything in him was screaming to go inside and *take.*

Who was he kidding? She'd claw his eyes out. And wasn't it painfully funny how the thought of fighting past her defenses to the passionate woman beneath made the blood in his arteries sting with the urge to battle through and conquer.

This was the problem. His primitive self, so unpredictable and given to self-destruction, wanted things that were no good for anyone.

He drove back to Milan in a state of unrest, trying to convince himself it was for the best that she hated him. Maybe Ryan had been a cheat, but it didn't make sleeping with the man's wife okay. It didn't mean Lauren was telling the truth about the baby.

Wallowing in his foul mood, he cursed passionately over tiny inconveniences like his shirt bringing the hanger with it as he pulled it off the rung. His cuff buttons refused to release and then, as he finally removed the shirt he was wearing, Lauren's mobile phone dropped out of his shirt pocket onto the carpet. He stared at it for a long moment, striving for control, then eventually swore tiredly.

Searching out the number for the villa, he called her. It rang four times before she answered cautiously, *"Buenasera."*

"It's me. I have your mobile. I'll bring it out tomorrow," he told her.

Nothing.

"Lauren?"

She swallowed audibly and said a strained, "I'm sleeping," then hung up on him.

She wasn't sleeping. She was crying. *Damn you, Ryan.*

Damn himself. He shouldn't have left her like that, but the last time he'd tried to comfort her—

Dio! What an untenable situation. Why hadn't he said something to Ryan at least? Chastised him?

Because he hadn't seen Ryan more than three or four times since that night. Occasionally he had received an email reading something like, Hey Buddy, I have a layover in Amsterdam. Come by for a beer? It was even more seldom that Paolo had been able to make it.

When they had sat down, it had been a rehash of glory days and whatever chances Ryan was taking on his missions and ruthless ribbing about how staid and responsible Paolo had become. They were both well past the age when they bragged about women, so the topic was avoided. Still, all the wild talk out of Ryan had often left Paolo wondering when his friend would grow up.

Ryan hadn't had to, he supposed. That was the major difference between the two of them. Losing his father had been a lesson in mortality for Paolo, one that Ryan had never taken seriously despite watching comrades fall around him. Ryan had lived in a bubble of belief that he was free from impact no matter what he did.

And Paolo had perpetuated that belief by not challenging him on his betrayal of Lauren. Lauren's asking for a divorce, questioning his fidelity, would have been Ryan's first hint that he wasn't as golden and untouchable as he'd come to believe. Thinking she was responsible for Ryan's death was a burden Lauren didn't deserve to bear. Paolo, the best friend, should have been the one to instill in Ryan that actions had consequences. If anyone was to blame for Ryan losing his life, it was Paolo. He should have made him see it was possible.

Instead he'd enabled Ryan to cheat on his wife, perpetuating Ryan's belief that Lauren would never know and so wouldn't be hurt by it. Perhaps Ryan had even operated under the certainty *he* would never be hurt by it.

Because his heart hadn't been as deeply involved as his wife's?

Disturbed, Paolo stroked his thumb on the cool black screen of Lauren's phone. Ryan had *loved*

Lauren, hadn't he? Whenever Paolo had asked about her, his friend had always smiled with deep satisfaction. Smug, almost.

Frustrated, Paolo shrugged on his clean shirt and slid her phone into his pocket. He didn't know why he kept it with him, just wanted the connection to her even though it was like wearing a badge of dishonor. His mood grew even more dour once he reached his aunt and uncle's house. Isabella's absence was noted by all and Vittorio was determined to make the most of it.

"What happened, Paolo? A spat over your dancing with Mrs. Bradley last night? I don't blame Isabella. Mrs. Bradley's a stunner. And *not* the woman I saw with our old friend in Berlin."

"No?" Paolo said shortly, impatient with the way the Bradleys were overtaking every minute of his life.

"Definitely not." Vittorio shook his head. "What kind of *coglione* deceives a woman like that?"

Lauren followed the dirty fingernail as it traced the train route on the map, listening carefully to broken French and Italian heavily laced with Spanish. The wind kept trying to pick up the map so she moved her empty espresso cup onto the corner. Its saucer clinked on the metal table of the al fresco café right before a screech of braking tires and a car horn scattered the nearby pigeons in a discordant mass of flapping wings and cooed protests.

As the birds cleared, Lauren saw Paolo leaving his car in the middle of the road, slamming the door as though it was a perfectly good parking space. The driver behind him shook his fist and shouted abuse.

"Go around," Paolo barked in Italian, keeping his gaze fixed on Lauren. When he was close enough, he set his fists on the map and leaned low enough to be eye to eye with her. "What are you doing here?"

Despite his level tone, she could practically taste the antagonism rolling off him. He was furious and she had no idea why. *She* was the injured party.

She sat back, repositioning her cheeky new hat over her shorn head so she could see him better. "Is that a philosophical question? Why am I on earth? Because I think it's quite obvious I'm at this café for coffee and directions."

His expression grew more dour, stirring an imaginary flock of birds in her belly. It took all her strength to hold his gaze when inside she was frantically rebuilding her self-worth. She could take acts of malice from jealous nobodies like her stepsiblings, but Paolo's dishonesty had burned like a dose of poison, spreading an ache to every corner of her body, leaving her distraught. She had thought she could trust him.

Through her haze of disillusionment, one festering question throbbed: why had he done it? Did he hate her that much?

She looked away, brows pleating. Why did she even want to trust him? She didn't need him. She was self-sufficient.

If she kept telling herself that, she might even believe it.

"Directions to where?" he asked, scanning the map.

"Venice," she murmured, unable to sound as enthused as she wanted to be. "Dino here tells me I should see it along with Rome, Naples, Pompeii... He started in Palermo."

Paolo turned his head long enough to say bluntly to her companion, "Leave us," before he lifted his Neanderthal knuckles off the map. Folding his arms, he ignored Lauren's mouth as she hung it open at his audacity.

"Why are you here and not at the villa? You knew I was coming," he said.

"And you thought I'd have tea and cookies waiting? I assumed you'd leave my phone on the hall table. Believe it or not, I wasn't keen to see you. Please stay to finish your coffee, Dino. *Gracias.*" She stood to gather her things, determined to end this by separating herself from Paolo swiftly and cleanly. "You're creating a jam," she pointed out. People were looking and she'd never been comfortable at the center of attention.

"Why didn't you use the car in the garage?" He took her bags with proprietary ease, leaving her scrambling to hang on to her purse at least.

"I felt like walking, but it was cooler than I expected. Hence the new hat."

"If you'd taken the car, I would have known you were shopping and wouldn't have run through the house like a madman, yelling for you. Don't do that again, Lauren."

To cover how disturbed she was by that revelation, she snorted, "When would I have occasion to? After this we really are never going to see each other again." She meant it. Keeping Ryan's secret and making her feel a fool was unforgivable.

He said nothing as he stowed her bags in the space behind the driver's seat.

Rather than argue, she said haughtily, "Leave everything on the front step," and started to turn away. This was painful enough, hating him while still reacting to every little flex and shift of his powerful body.

"Get in the car, Lauren."

"I prefer to walk," she told him, using a cutting stare to drive home to him that she would die before she'd go anywhere with him.

"Do you want me to put you in it?" He pushed his seat into place with a sharp click and a meaningful gather of his muscled frame.

"You wouldn't. Not here," she scoffed with a little smile and shake of her head. A car crawled past, honking repeatedly.

"I will," he assured her. It wasn't so much his tone that gave her pause, despite it being very severe. It was the inferno of cold heat in his eyes, a maelstrom beneath his calm demeanor.

Her heart skipped a beat. She wasn't afraid of him, but for a second she was afraid of *it*. The energy. The source of his anger. It was an unknown force, but it felt very personal.

To combat it, she reminded herself he was a liar. He had held her in contempt for sleeping with him so soon after Ryan's death while fully aware that Ryan had been cheating all along. As her indignant fury soaked back into their staring contest, the spark of rebellion in her expanded to an inferno.

"Go for it," she goaded, and returned to the café and Dino's watchful curiosity.

Never in a million years would she have believed Paolo would do it, but athletic arms gathered her up faster than a parent caught a runaway toddler. The sudden grab startled her into letting out a yelp that turned into a string of angry protests as she wriggled in the cradle hold that pinned her to his chest.

He was beyond impervious. And strong. Amazingly strong since she was not only tall, but she'd started putting on baby pounds.

None of that made an impact and despite her struggles, he wasn't the least bit rough. He carried her around to the passenger side like she was a case of crystal tableware, prone to breakage.

Why that made her feel secure, she had no idea,

but for all the horrid embarrassment of being man-handled in public like this, there was a component of sweetness. She loved being close to him again. Feeling the ripple of his flexing muscles made her go weak with anticipation…

That would be embarrassing. She began to struggle more earnestly, but he didn't set her on her feet until he needed to free one hand to open the car door.

She glared at him, flushed and hot. Shaking off his grip on her arm, she said, "You made my hat fall off!"

"Get in or I'll run over your damned hat."

He would. She could see he was in just that sort of rancorous mood.

Fuming, she plopped into the car and buckled up, watching as he circled the car, snatched up her hat, then threw it across to her as he climbed behind the wheel.

"What is wrong with you?" she muttered as she gently pinched the felt brim back into shape.

"*You* are wrong with me," he bit out, squealing his tires as he peeled away like they were leaving a bank robbery. "I haven't behaved so outrageously in years, but you had to throw down the gauntlet, didn't you?"

"You didn't have to pick it up!"

"I was worried about you," he near shouted. "You fainted two days ago, in case you've forgotten. I thought I'd find you facedown in the pool. Instead you were flirting with some transient. I wasn't about to leave you to make your own way home and not know if you made it. What if he followed you?"

"He's a grad student on break—"

"I don't care who he is. Don't talk to strangers." He pulled into the villa's drive, reducing her leisurely twenty-minute walk to half a minute with his arrogant, caveman foot on the gas.

"Strangers like you? Because you sure aren't the man I gave you credit for being!"

He said nothing, just braked to a firm stop and sat there with hollow cheeks, hands gripping the wheel of the car so hard his knuckles stood out white and sharp as the glaciers across the lake.

"I would ask you why you did it, but I already know. You hate me and Ryan was your best fr—"

"I thought something horrible had happened to you today! Does that sound like I hate you? Look at my hands. They're still shaking." He showed her one that was a hair off rock steady. "What does that tell you?"

"That you're a really good actor."

CHAPTER SIX

SHE SLAMMED OUT of the car and went into the house. He followed, aware that he'd already revealed too much, but he couldn't leave things like this.

"Stupid electronic locks," she muttered with a baleful glance when he entered. "I'm looking for the manual, you know. I'm going to change the number."

"You didn't answer when I called out to you." He set her shopping bags on the sofa. "I knew you were upset last night. I shouldn't have left you like that." Paolo ran a hand down his face trying to erase those few minutes of recalled terror when he couldn't find her in this house. "You have no idea what that was like. None."

"You honestly thought I had drowned myself in despair? I'm not depressed, Paolo. I'm angry. So angry you can't even imagine. And where can I let it out? On a dead man? No one wants to hear that the Great American Hero was a common cheat. If they did, all those women who slept with him and all those men who knew about it would be saying something, but they're not! They want their mythical hero."

She gestured expansively as she spoke, animating the full injustice. "Meanwhile, I get to maintain the lie. I get to look like the dopey wife who didn't have a clue, and in six months, I get to look like the inconstant spouse. Thanks to you."

Lauren's pointed finger of accusation could have been a bullet, Paolo felt it go through him so tangibly.

"If you were the least bit worried about me, you'd take responsibility and help me through all of this." Her voice grew jagged. "But you just want me to quit making life difficult for you. Well, happy day for you, I'm going south and you can forget I exist."

If only, he thought while "No" formed like a diamond inside him. He spoke it quietly and without compromise. *Dio!* If she met up with another smooth-talking backpacker who thought he could get lucky with her—

Paolo had hit a wall when he'd seen her nestled so close to the stranger, her pixie face as trusting as ever, the young man dazzled and eager. Paolo had already been frantic and that had been a new threat he was completely unwilling to tolerate. Another man in her life? *Like hell.*

He instinctively knew the action he wanted to take to curtail such a thing, but he had spent years training himself not to react from his gut. Better to look at this from all sides first.

"You're not the boss of me, Paolo." Lauren carried her bags to the kitchen island and began putting away the contents. "If I want to go, I'll go."

True, he didn't have much influence over her and that needed to change. This was a turning point. Keeping her at a distance was not working. Hiding her away was a temporary measure at best. He'd been reacting out of shock since she'd ambushed him in New York, but her pregnancy would be discovered. His reputation would need triage no matter whether the baby turned out to be his or not.

He still shied from embracing the baby as his own. Logically he knew it was not only possible but probable, but his heart would not let down its guard. A large part of that was his reluctance to trust Lauren—or rather himself. Believing could turn out to be wishful thinking born out of how susceptible he was to her.

For some reason his libido caught fire at the mere thought of her. Despite their argument yesterday, he'd barely slept as he relived Charleston. She wasn't exactly dressed to entice today, wearing a knitted pullover and fresh jeans, but the blue cables draped softly over her narrow shoulders and thrusting breasts, while the jeans cupped her bottom faithfully, giving her a leggy yet curvy silhouette that drew his eye and held it.

He wanted her and it wasn't going away. Possessing her in Charleston had made the hunger worse, not better. If she hadn't been pregnant, a quiet, lengthy affair would have been the perfect solution, but she *was* pregnant. And alone.

He had nothing but contempt for men who refused to take responsibility for their children. Standing on high ground knowing he wasn't the father would be cold comfort if Lauren wound up raising her child alone while the world judged Paolo as the deadbeat who'd put her in that position. No, he couldn't take that risk with his reputation and, frankly, wouldn't be able to live with himself if he cut her off simply because the baby wasn't his. If she had fallen into a dead-end affair just before Ryan disappeared, it was because she'd been lonely, grieving over the loss of her grandmother and scorned by her unfaithful husband.

Whose fault was it that she'd still been in that marriage? He kept coming back to that. *If you were the least bit worried about me, you'd take responsibility and help me through all of this.*

He couldn't deny that he'd been worried about her. The depth of his worry unnerved him, making him expect a cold sweat to condense over him as he let himself contemplate tying himself to her permanently. Instead, the mist seemed to clear from his mind while a weight lifted away. Marriage. *Si.* It was the perfect solution. His gut knew it and so did his intellect.

"If you give me a few days to make arrangements," he said with placating calm, "I can take you south myself. We'll call it a honeymoon."

Lauren subtly slid one hand over the other, pinching the back of her hand and giving it a fervent twist for good measure. Her heart tripped into a trot, a canter, then a gallop. It found an opening in the shields she usually kept in place against Paolo and raced toward him.

"Are you proposing?" Her voice wasn't quite steady as disbelief threatened to unbalance into spirit-swelling elation.

He stood taller, his stature filled with pride and masculine elegance. Her mind's eye took a photo of him like that: regal and handsome and projecting his will like a force that made her sway with admiration and primitive desire to capitulate.

"*Si,* that is exactly what I am doing. Proposing marriage."

A glow of jubilation warmed her. "You believe me about the baby, then?" Finally. She began to soften all over. A joyous smile tickled her lips.

His expression remained shuttered.

"That can be proven in time, but in the short term you need someone to watch out for you. Since I will be perceived as the father, I'll do what's expected—"

Her ears blocked out the rest. Her heart snapped back into her chest, doors slamming behind it. Everything in her was crushed and buried under disappointment and rejection. She turned back to her groceries to hide what a slap-down this was.

"Why would you do that again? Marry when you're not sure whether you're the father of the baby?" she choked out, keeping her head down, confused and appalled by how buoyant and excited she'd been at the prospect of him falling in love with her.

"This time I know there is doubt. And Ryan shouldn't have left you in a position of feeling you had to isolate yourself from people to hide his behavior. As his friend, it's my duty to look out for his wife. Did you not just tell me to take more responsibility?"

"Not because you think I'm some kind of charity case! I want you to take responsibility because you love and want your child." She wanted him to want *her*.

Recognizing that, realizing she was still the needy girl who had married in a rush in case Ryan changed his mind, made her want to break down into jet-lagged, hormone-provoked, hurt and angry tears. Mamie had told her a thousand times she could have everything she dreamed of if she would only believe she deserved it, but it was hard. Very hard when this man was offering a pity-marriage on the heels of his pity-bedding.

"I'm sure I'll come to care for the child no matter who fathered it. Which is something you will communicate to any man who might come forward in the future." Paolo's demeanor hardened right down to the pinpoints of his aggressively contracted pupils.

Her heart skipped a beat, startled by his sudden shift to undisguised possessiveness. His teeth showed in a subtle snarl.

"I'm going into this with my eyes open, but so are you. Once we tie the knot, you and the baby are mine. No take-backs." He withdrew her phone from his pocket and held it out to her. As though he expected her to call her mystery man and blurt out his reverse-ransom demands.

Lauren wanted to release a laugh of offended pride, but was afraid it would come out as a sob. She ignored the phone and held his stare with defiant refusal to move across the room and touch it while a sensation like falling down a mountain tumbled through her. Her voice hurt her throat when she managed to speak.

"No need. I won't marry a man who thinks it's okay to cheat."

His head recoiled like she'd slapped him. He

tightened his grip on her phone until she thought the screen would crack. "I don't cheat."

"I wish I could believe you, Paolo, but you've lied to me before." Her hand shook as she went back to stowing groceries in the refrigerator. "Men like you are incapable of monogamy."

"Men like me?"

"Like you and Ryan. You're sex machines. You made a pass at a bride on her wedding day, for God's sake!"

"And you kissed me back," he near shouted. "You came out to the garden after me, so don't make out like I hunted you down. I was trying to get away from you. You made the first move in Charleston, too. So which one of us is the sex machine?"

Before she knew what she was doing, the yellow tomato left her hand and was flying at his head.

He fielded it like a pro, his reflexes catlike. His reaction of astonished disbelief came more slowly as he looked at the orb smashed into his palm. Very deliberately he set it aside and wiped his hand on his shirt, lifting his head in a way of a predator locking onto his prey. Retribution was a ferocious light in his outraged expression.

Lauren's heart stopped. All her blood drained into her toes and a cold sweat chased it. She was as flabbergasted as he was and the way he seemed to gather and glow with challenge melted her into a puddle of apprehension.

"I—I—" she stammered.

He began walking toward her and she tried to retreat, backing into the fridge door and knocking condiments over in their trays while her nerveless fingers lost their grip on the cloth bag. It fell to the floor. More tomatoes rolled out toward his menacing steps while she managed to shuffle around the door and clatter it closed, taking refuge at one end of the island, putting it between them as he came up to the other end, threat in every line of his aggressive stance.

Part of her knew this standoff was insanely childish, but he looked not just furious, but intent. She was trapped and a frisson of something unidentifiable went through her. Not real fear, but the kind that chased you through a haunted house, making you want to laugh while you were screaming your head off.

"What are you doing hiding behind furniture? You wanted a fight, didn't you?" he taunted in a voice that sent a sensual slither down her spine. "Or were you inviting something else?"

"I was inviting you to get lost, but you can't stand for a woman to resist you, can you?" She practically threw the words out.

"If you at least tried to resist, *cara,* we might not be in this situation."

"Who is chasing who right now? I don't want anything to do with you. You're behaving like an idiot."

His head went back in insult while a hint of desperation shadowed the eyes that stayed fixed on her. "Do I really have to chase a woman who wants to be caught?"

Her heart did a backflip while she protested, "Get over yourself!"

At the same time her heart raced with something more like anticipation than fear, even though she was very scared how she'd react if he touched her.

He made a sudden fake to her left. She feinted in a mirror dodge that started him down one side of the island. She took her chances running down the opposite side.

Paolo was not only competitive, but strong, athletic, and ruthless. Before she'd taken four steps, he had vaulted onto and slid over the island, landing before her so she would have crashed into him if he hadn't caught her by the arms to cushion the impact.

"You—"

He smothered her cry of anger with his mouth.

She shouldn't have been shocked. He was cutthroat enough to prove a point in this ruthless way, even if he did hate her. He didn't have to resort to violence when he could demean her with her own uncontrollable response to him.

The devastating crush of his mouth on hers was a stamp of ownership, one full of all-knowing familiarity. He took for granted he'd elicit a response, and he did. Despite her admonishments to herself that she ought to fight him, should bite his bottom lip and beat her fists on his chest, something deeply vulnerable gave way inside her.

Weak tears smarted at the backs of her eyes, but they came from wanting this so badly and knowing it was nothing but a point to be proven for him while she was flowering like a desert plant tasting water after a drought. With an internal shudder, she gave in to him.

He groaned in victory and maneuvered her into a closer alignment with his hard angles, backing her into the fridge so he could press his weight into her.

She released a sigh of deep relief and she climbed her hands up to his neck, weaving her fingers into his short, silky hair, encouraging him with the pressure of her touch against his warm scalp to kiss her harder. Deeper. She opened her mouth unreservedly to his and their tongues tangled in delicious reunion.

It wasn't enough. When he nudged his knee between her thighs, she let him in, giving over to his natural need to dominate without a second thought. She ached to feel him take over her body.

He ceased massaging her hip to slither his touch restlessly into her clothing. His expertise made her heart contract with both delight and a poignant awareness of how practiced he was. She broke out in shivery bumps from the sweet caress of his palm over her navel, measuring the expansion of her waistline before he stroked up her rib cage.

He was only going through the motions to taunt her, she reminded herself. It was galling to be so incapable of resisting him, but she couldn't escape the grip of desire for his touch. She wanted to weep, she felt so defenseless.

He growled something approving as his hand splayed over the growing abundance of her breast. Unerringly, he found her nipple with his thumb, circling and inciting sensations through the cup of her bra that were so intense they were almost painful. Lauren groaned in protest and wriggled against him. Paolo firmed his hold on her and intensified their kiss while he slid his touch inside her bra, his caress the work of a connoisseur that brought the tip to a screaming pitch of sensitivity.

Unbelievably, a shower of tingling sensations raced down her abdomen and into her loins, gathering into a knot of joyful anticipation. She clenched internal muscles, trying to resist what was happening, but her body knew what it wanted.

She was going to climax right here, fully clothed in the kitchen.

Aghast, she fought free of his kiss and covered his hand to still his fingers, gasping, "Paolo, stop. Now. Please."

"I adore the way you feel when you're aroused, *cara.*" His strong hand resisted the stilling press of her own while his breath stirred the hair at her temple, fanning the burning need inside her. "*Dio!* I've never known a woman so responsive. Let me take you to bed."

"No!" She covered her face to hide that she was near tears and pivoted away, leaning her shoulder heavily into the cold wall of the fridge door, dislodging his touch so his hand fell to her waist. He continued to stand behind her, his grip twitching through degrees of strength on the sensitized skin of her waist, as though he wanted to grip her harder and was fighting the urge. Desire to turn back into him nearly overwhelmed her.

"Lauren, you want this. You want *me*."

"But I don't want to prove I'm the easiest woman you've ever met! What a horrid thing to say to someone. Shall I tell you how you rank in *my* vast experience?"

His hand dropped away and he retreated a step so cool air swirled down her back, making her shiver. "That isn't what I was saying."

"Yes, you were. You kissed me to prove I can't control how I react to you, and that's just mean. I've tried not to be attracted to you, Paolo. God knows I've tried. I know I behaved badly in Charleston. That's why I don't expect you to marry me. But taking advantage of my weakness so you can notch your belt is not nice. And refusing to admit Ryan was cheating was cruel. I could be divorced and married to a man who genuinely loves me, expecting *his* child, rather than wading through this mess."

Paolo took everything she said like a series of heart punches, taken aback by her claim that he was only toying with her. Did she really not have any idea how powerfully attracted to her he was? He might have been a playboy once, but this wasn't like that.

Yet he'd thought the same of her. He'd written off her signals of interest as deliberate flirtation, but as he looked at the back of her bowed neck, so vulnerable and conquered, he remembered the innocent who'd sat beside him in a bar five years ago, so uncomfortable with her own sexuality she'd never stopped tugging at her short skirt or low neckline.

He suddenly saw the truth. Lauren had been fighting this same attraction he'd been struggling against for the very same reason: they'd had spouses to consider.

That he'd been so successful in hiding the true depth of his attraction took him aback, especially today. She ought to realize by twenty-five how alluring she was.

Unless her husband had never been home to tell

her. If said husband had done the exact opposite, stayed away and had affairs, it was no shock at all that Lauren would have little awareness of her appeal.

Remorse moved through Paolo. He knew how it felt to be lied to. His trust in women was skewed to this day, nearly impossible to win. Apparently, Lauren was equally suspicious and he didn't like how unsteady that made him feel.

Paolo tipped back his head for a cleansing breath before moving away from her to fetch two glasses from the cupboard. When he came back to use the ice machine on the door of the refrigerator, Lauren eyed him warily and sidled to make room.

He filled one with filtered water and handed it to her. For himself, he reached into another cupboard where the hard liquor was kept and poured something from the first bottle that came to hand. It spilled through him in a bracing burn, not cooling his blood, but clearing his mind enough that he could think.

And all he could think was that he had to have her.

First, though, he had to erase that haunted, white-lipped look off her face. She looked dazed and shell-shocked. Tension outlined her eyes, keeping her gaze from meeting his, and she choked a little as she sipped her water.

"I knew you were a virgin before I spoke to you," he told her.

She darted a confused look his way, her brow crinkling briefly with annoyance. "Don't rub it in. I know I'm not sophisticated. Did you have a good laugh with Ryan?"

"Quite the opposite. I was afraid for you. That's why I approached you. To keep the creeps in that bar from taking advantage of you."

That's what he'd told himself anyway, using it to justify a drink with a stranger when he was about to marry another woman. He thumbed the rim of his glass.

"You don't have a clue how striking you are, do you? That men want you? That backpacker, for instance?" He jerked his head in the direction of the village.

She snorted, shaking her head in dismissal. "He wanted a shower and a clean bed. He wanted to use me for that."

"Case in point," he muttered, letting her see his

mild disgust, not the least bit reassured by her faint blush and frown of suspicion.

"You're teasing me."

"No, Lauren, I'm being as honest as I know how. Did you hear the part where I said I was trying to get away from you at your wedding? I've *always* wanted you."

CHAPTER SEVEN

LAUREN HELD HIS gaze until the dark centers of his eyes seemed to glow with heat. Her toes curled and emotion welled up in her, bursting for release.

Alarmed, she looked away and reminded herself to draw a breath. With a dry swallow, she escaped by crouching to pick up the scattered groceries.

"I find that hard to believe. For starters, you're a man who enjoys a challenge and I don't present much of one. As you pointed out, I was the one chasing you at the wedding." Cringing at the memory, she squinted her eyes shut. The cloth bag rested in a heap on her thigh. "I didn't go out there to kiss you, though. Please believe that, Paolo. You were just so angry and upset and I felt like it was my fault you had to witness a wedding when it was the last thing you believed in anymore. I just wanted to see if you were okay."

"I wasn't." The husky edge on his voice fluttered her nerves with disturbing sensuality.

"I know. It was stupid of me to ask." She shook out the bag and filled it with the produce she gathered.

"No, it was kind, Lauren. It was sweet and I repaid you by kissing you and asking you to leave with me. *That* was stupid."

She stayed on her knees, tilting only her eyes up to the man towering over her, his broad shoulders heavy with self-recrimination.

"You didn't want to be there. It was an imposition. You wanted to be left alone and I didn't respect that, so you gave me a mental shake."

"No," he contradicted very gravely. "I was serious when I asked you to leave with me. I went outside to cool my head because I'd been watching you all day. When you followed me, I gave in to temptation. If you had slapped me, I would have backed off, but—"

"I know. I'm—" She curled hands that rose to cover her face, leaving her fists against her hot cheeks while she stared up at him in hypnotic chagrin. To this day she remembered every second of the way he'd turned, his expression pained and defeated. She'd instinctively reached out and he'd caught her hand and drawn her inexorably into him.

She hadn't recognized they were going to kiss. It had just happened. He had covered her mouth with his and pulled a response from her that shattered everything she'd known about herself. Still hovering between the girl who wondered about sex and the young woman awakening to her own sexuality, she'd suddenly glimpsed the raw power inside herself and it had scared her. Truly scared her.

As she'd pulled back, he'd feathered a masculine command across her lips. *Vieni con me.*

She'd understood the Italian words as though it was her primary language and the desire to comply had been dangerously thick in her blood. *Leave with me.*

And then Ryan's chilly voice had asked, "What are you doing?"

For one heartbeat Paolo's grip on her had tightened. She'd understood what it meant to be a kill between two hungry wolves.

Or a female between two alphas.

Her domestic breeding had kicked in at that point and she'd suddenly seen what this looked like from the outside, from Ryan's perspective and the handful of family who'd gathered behind him. A bride in her lace regalia embracing another man, her lips still swollen from the pressure of his kiss, her cheeks flushed with arousal.

She'd been appalled with herself and quickly done everything in her power to excuse and minimize what had happened. Paolo was drunk. He was angry at marriage and her, and was expressing it by messing with her.

And she had moved back to Ryan's side because he was the safe choice. When he kissed her, she felt a warm glow, not like she was falling into the lava of an erupting volcano. Ryan only came as far into her heart as she let him; Paolo would steal it and own it and probably break it.

Lauren lowered her gaze, trying to believe she'd made the right choice that day even though it smacked of severe cowardice.

"I'm trying to quit apologizing all the time, but I really didn't mean to behave like that." His ego didn't need to hear that yet another female was gaga over him. "I don't know what came over me, letting you kiss me like that."

"Lust," he said pointedly, making her heart dip with horrid embarrassment, as if a protective veil had been yanked away to reveal her nudity. Then he added, "I'd like to blame my kissing you on my broken marriage or the fact my father had passed away two weeks before, but you and I have chemistry, Lauren."

A spike of pleasurable heat clenched in her belly. She wanted to look away, so self-conscious her skin hurt, but she hung on every word.

"That doesn't excuse asking you to leave with me, though. Who the hell does that? To his *best friend?* I was sick with myself when Ryan caught us. It never should have happened and I swore to him it never would again."

Finally her gaze dropped to the floor, but she didn't see anything but the cold, distant looks Paolo had been throwing her ever since. That was why. Their night in Charleston had broken that promise and he was a man who didn't break promises.

"My marriage, everything about my relationship with my ex-wife, was a trail of arrogant decisions," he muttered. "My situation at the time, giving up what I wanted in order to take over the bank, couldn't be turned to my advantage. I didn't want to believe it and, yes, wanted to assert my own will, but throwing away common sense and kissing you was the wrong way to do it. I damaged a lifelong friendship and knew I had to make changes within myself."

Her stomach twisted in anxiety. Paolo was far too competitive to lose, especially to himself. That determination to master himself meant he would fight showing further weakness where she was concerned. He didn't want to be attracted to her. It galled him. Lessened him.

She felt tears smart behind her eyes, not wanting to be an instrument of his downfall. He would always resent her for it.

"After behaving like that at his wedding, what would Ryan have thought a few years later if I had told you that yes, I suspected he was cheating?" Paolo asked with quiet fervor. "I didn't have proof. He would have thought I was making a play for you, especially because I could hardly keep my eyes off you that night, either. If you hadn't gone home early and left us to drink ourselves blind, I don't know what I would have done. All I knew was that I couldn't destroy his marriage."

The admission held so much bitterness, she flinched. Her fingers were numb and icy, her legs stiff and aching as she stood and set the bag on the island, not looking at Paolo as she digested his rationalizations for not telling her the truth.

"I felt guilty, too," she acknowledged. "I had kissed you back and shouldn't have. That's why I talked myself out of believing he was cheating a million times, dismissing certain signs..." She drew a long, deep breath and released it in a grievous sigh. "Sometimes things happen that shouldn't. I knew that."

"*Esattamente.* Sometimes there is a physical connection that can't be helped."

Pressure built behind Lauren's eyes as she kept her gaze fixed across the room, not wanting Paolo to see that for her, it wasn't strictly physical. There was an emotional component of attraction and admiration and desire to be noticed and valued. She wanted him to feel something for her besides unwanted sexual attraction.

She swallowed.

"Is it—?" She cleared the throb from her voice. "If you're just reacting because it's been a while—"

"It has been a while," he stated flatly. "Since our night in Charleston, if you want the truth, and that's damned near a record for me."

A stinging blush hit her cheeks. "Another one

of your charming Italian compliments? Try being married to a man in the military. There were nights I wished I *was* capable of an affair."

A dangerous light came into his black-coffee eyes. He approached her and she retreated a step, halting when his eyes narrowed.

"No, don't run, *tesoro*. We know where that leads." His smile was wicked, almost cruel.

Lauren held her ground, lifting her chin even though it exposed the sensitive place in her throat where her pulse began pounding so hard it threatened to burst her skin. Clutching the edge of the island behind her, she stood very still as his hand came up to cradle her jaw.

"No, it's not just abstinence making me feel this way," he stated gruffly. "This is not a fleeting thing. It needs a long-term arrangement. Physical desire would not be the worst basis for a marriage, you must admit that."

Her jaw hardened as he spoke, growing more rocklike by the second as she saw how he was leading her down the path he wanted her to go. He stroked her skin with lightly splayed fingers, persuading her to soften, and much of her wanted to. The desire to give in was a whisper away.

But she was acutely aware he'd said nothing about feelings, nothing about creating a family with the baby they'd made. He wanted a bedmate. That was all.

"You understand now why I was less than honest with you," he cajoled gently. "You can believe me when I tell you I will be entirely monogamous. Why would I stray when the best is at home?"

She jerked away from his hold, lowering her eyes to hide how badly she wanted to believe him. All of her longed for a husband who gave her children and came home to her and their family every day. Maybe she was trying to rewrite her childhood when she'd been surrounded by "real" families while she was the odd duck whose father had died and whose step-siblings resented her. But the yearning in her to have a nuclear family was intense and real.

Without love, however, there would be no glue. If sex was all that brought a man home, it could lead him afield just as easily. And if there was even a seed of suspicion between them…

"Whether I trust you is only half the equation, isn't it? You don't trust me."

Silence. His hand lowered and balled into a fist of frustration.

"If I am the father, Lauren, you would not refuse to marry me," he finally said.

"So marrying you would prove to you that you are? That's what you're saying?" She flung back her head.

She could see by his expression it wouldn't be that easy, only that refusing to marry him would, in his eyes, prove once and for all that he wasn't the father.

She jerked conflicted eyes to the blurred panes of glass on the cupboards, brow knotting in pain. "You're not being fair," she murmured, hurt that he refused to take her word.

He lightly caressed her cheek with his knuckle. "Lauren."

She leaned away from his touch. "Don't. Getting your way like that will make me hate you."

Paolo tensed, feeling as though heavy chains were settling and binding around him. Lauren had been beyond his grasp for too long for him to accept distance now.

"Don't be stubborn," he growled, frustrated that she refused to see what a chance he was taking in offering marriage without a guarantee about the baby's paternity.

"You're the one being stubborn," she accused, crackling with the passionate energy that lit such a fire in him.

"I have to take a long view," he reminded.

"Well, I'm not about to rush headlong into marriage without considering all the ramifications, either. I married the first time because I thought it was my only option. My mother had brainwashed me into thinking I *needed* a man in my life. I don't. When the baby is born, you can take blood tests. Let me know then if you want to be involved, and we'll discuss marriage."

"And you'll vilify my reputation in the meantime. Very nice," he bit out.

Lauren rotated to face him with feminine aggression. "If you think you can change my mind by telling me your job is more important than my happiness, you're wrong. Been there, done that. Tell me what I will get out of marriage and I'll think about it."

Hellfire, she was beautiful. The short hair worked for her, exposing a face that glowed with passion and assertiveness. That force tapped an answering signal in him, making him want to frame her face in his hands and kiss the hell out of her. They were both still aroused. That's why they were on the verge of killing each other, snapping like territorial dogs. If she thought he wasn't aware of the points of her nipples turgid against the fall of her light sweater, she was kidding herself. All he could think about was how close he'd had her to orgasm simply by fondling her breast. It took all his self-control not to adjust the ache behind his fly, but he was afraid that if he touched himself, he'd give in, open his pants and have her on the floor.

She knew what was going on in his mind. Her breathing pattern hitched and her lips parted invitingly while her body language grew soft and receptive.

He smiled. "You want the sex as much as I do, *cara*. Marry me."

"I'm not as uptight as I used to be, Paolo. I can have sex without a ring."

He let his brows go up, not liking that supercilious note in her voice. It was too suggestive of confidence that she could manage him. "You think?" he challenged.

She snorted. "I may be easy, but so are you."

He folded his arms, taking full advantage of his height to look down on her. "And if I told you I won't make love to you until my ring is on your finger?"

"Really?" A smile of genuine amusement grew across her lips. "You want to take that on as a challenge or a bet or whatever it is your crazy, competitive nature drinks in as fuel? You have a streak of perversity, you know that? Okay, run with it. Let's see how far you get." She chuckled and turned away to reach for her water, turning back with the glass raised nearly to her grin before adding, "Keeping in mind that I can have sex whenever and with whomever I choose."

"Oh, that's where you are wrong, *cara*. Very, very wrong."

He hemmed her in with long arms braced on either side of her. Flutters of heat fanned the desire simmering inside him, but his ego was fully on the line now. He wouldn't make love to her until he had what he wanted: her. And he was the only man who would touch her ever again.

"I'm not coming back to another empty house and having a heart attack because you're down the road flirting with university dropouts. You and I will be joined at the hip until you agree to marry me, sharing this house or staying in the city to see my family—which is where we are going tonight. Do you have something to wear or shall we go shopping?"

Lauren was gearing up to tell him to back off and get real, but her inner diva heard the magic word and went, *O-oh, shopping.* The suitcases upstairs were half empty and she had high intentions of filling them.

Paolo straightened and nodded. "Shopping it is."

"Wait! That wasn't agreement."

"You want to know what marriage to me offers, do you not? Allow me to show you how you are treated when you are related to the most powerful banker in Milan. And you will agree to dinner. I would like my mother to know about us before the rumors start. Because they will."

The assumption in that phrase "know about us" got her back up, but it was overshadowed by the resignation in his tone. Lauren shivered. She wanted to be as confident as she managed to sound about having her baby alone, but deep down she was as fragile and uncertain as any new mother.

She longed for support she could count on, just not when it was being offered so reluctantly.

And despite the kisses they'd shared today and his claim that he was attracted to her, she was genuinely gun-shy about rushing into another marriage that was only trying to serve convention.

Getting out of the house suddenly sounded like an ideal distraction from dwelling on problems they couldn't resolve.

Paolo had to give Lauren credit. As a man who had escorted countless women through the fashion houses in Milan—relatives, mistresses, his first wife—he was very familiar with where to go and whom to see. His own clothes were tailored almost exclusively by Corneliani; the son of his father's tailor had been making Paolo's suits since Paolo had been a ring bearer for Vittorio's parents at three. Nevertheless, Paolo knew where they were headed even before Lauren seated herself next to him, placed two hands over the pocketbook she set on her knees and said with breathless anticipation, "Via Monte Napoleone, please."

He privately smirked. She was a natural when

it came to learning what a wealthy banker offered a woman.

Being wanted for his money didn't bother him. He knew it was part of the package along with his looks and his position in society. He was secure enough to know his own worth apart from those trappings and, to be honest, was just as superficial when it came to singling out a woman. He liked the beautiful ones and if they possessed a sharp wit, all the better. None had ever made him ache with desire quite the way Lauren did, which unnerved him a little, but he was coming around to accepting it.

Marriage. The more he thought about it, the more determined he was to make it happen. There was something enormously satisfying in the image of her wearing his ring and standing by his side.

He still couldn't believe she'd thrown a tomato at him though. What a virago! It made him want to laugh even as he recognized he'd have to tame that streak out of her. Who would have guessed so much emotion and passion had been stifled under that curtain of hair she'd been wearing all her life? He was incredibly stimulated by it—dangerously so. He feared it would feed into his own wildness.

Stifling it in both of them could pose quite a challenge.

There would be compensations for tempering it, though. He took care to demonstrate that by saying to the woman who greeted them at the design house, "Lauren will need a page in the Donatelli account."

"Of course, *signore,*" the woman said with a subtle shift of heightened respect and closer attention to her new client. "Is the *signorina* looking for anything in particular today?"

Lauren broke from her absorption of her surroundings to say in Italian, "I'm looking at everything. But, Paolo, don't be silly. If there's one place my grandmother would want me to spend her money, it would be here. She worked as a model for this house in the seventies," Lauren added in an aside to the woman, moving deeper into the room with the awe most people saved for the frescoed ceilings of his country's renowned cathedrals. "Did you ever hear of Frances Hammond?"

Within moments Paolo's wealth and name had been trumped by the mysterious quilting of intergenerational female relationships. Their hostess rushed to phone for refreshments while designers emerged from back rooms to coo over their special visitor.

Paolo left Lauren in their capable hands, spending a quiet hour at his office where half the staff had stolen away to Christmas shop. When he returned, he found Lauren so happy he stood arrested for a long moment.

She'd completed her transformation from widowed wife to a confident woman of means. Her yellow-brown eyes were sparkling, set off by a green-and-gold scarf knotted around her slender neck. Her smart tunic dress was straight enough, and loose enough, to disguise that her waist was thickening and she distracted from that area with a pair of chic, four-inch heels.

He realized that it hadn't been hair weighing down her personality all these years. It had been lack of joie de vivre. Here was her true spirit in all its glory, and she stopped his breath.

Mine, he thought, but restrained himself from a possessive kiss. Everyone was now calling her "Signora Bradley." The cat had a claw out of the bag.

He made arrangements for delivery of her purchases to the house on Lake Como, subtly signaled that Lauren's credit card receipt should be torn up and the balance put on his account as he had originally requested, then waited until they were alone in the car to ask, "Did you tell them you're pregnant?"

"Of course not!" Lauren angled toward Paolo, aware of his gaze flickering to her bare knees. A pleasurable warmth swished through her, making her feel beautiful and confident, something that had been wavering since meeting him again in New York. This visit with women who had subtly reminded her of all the qualities her grandmother had possessed had reinvigorated her toward believing she could get there, too.

With a brush of her wispy bangs to the side, she said, "They kept remarking on my weight though. I finally explained I'd been sick earlier in the year and lost a lot and when I made a point of gaining it back, I went overboard."

"What is it with women? You're healthy," he protested. "But were you genuinely sick? I remember thinking you were too thin when I saw you in Charleston."

"Depressed. After losing Mamie I didn't have to make regular meals anymore. I thought Ryan would ask me to jump on a plane any day, so I kept the groceries low. Then I got that woman's email and the fighting started. My stomach was in knots."

Paolo's heart jerked. He took his foot off the accelerator and drew a subtle breath, focusing on keeping both of them alive in heavy traffic as he absorbed how rough a time Lauren had been through.

It bothered him that he'd known nothing about her anguish, but why should he have? His coping strategy had been to avoid her and he had. He was nevertheless deeply disturbed by the fact that she had needed her husband and Ryan hadn't responded.

"I'm sorry you lost her, Lauren. I don't think I've said that and it's always been apparent to me what she meant to you." He reached across and squeezed her hand, the sexual tension there but subdued. He was utterly sincere in his condolences.

Lauren squeezed back, but released him right away and he thought it was to keep her emotions under control. Her voice was thick as she said, "Losing her was really hard. She was always the one to pick me up when my stepfather's kids knocked me down."

"Physically? They hurt you?" His protective instincts gathered.

"Emotionally. My father died when I was six. Mom never worked outside the home so when the insurance money ran out she needed a husband to support her. Gerald worked in the oil patch and had three kids. He was away a lot and I guess he thought Mom filled the void. If they love each other, I've never seen it. His kids hated us being in their home and tortured us when Gerald wasn't there, calling me praying mantis and stealing my things. They were awful. My only relief was visiting Mamie, but Mom limited my time with her, afraid she'd poison me with self-assurance I guess. Although, Mamie could be a brat," Lauren confided with a grin of appreciation. "She spoiled me, sending me the latest gadgets and designer clothes. It's no wonder Gerald's kids hated me. They must have been jealous."

"I like her style," Paolo said with affection for a woman he'd only met once, but whose fragile, yet elegant beauty had left an impression.

"She liked yours," Lauren countered with a smirk. "Every time I came home from Charleston she'd ask, 'Did you see that sexy Italian from your wedding?'"

"What would she tell you to do now? Marry me?" Paolo challenged lightly.

Lauren was quiet a long time, then said to the side window, "She'd say don't marry for any reason but love. You don't want to be tied down when you find the person you're meant to be with."

CHAPTER EIGHT

DESPITE THE GRANDNESS of Paolo's ancestral home, it was very much that: a home. The villa was set behind an ornate gate on an expansive estate of fountains and sprawling trees, but children played in the hedge maze and men smoked on a terrace off the second floor. Winter pansies shivered in ceramic pots at the front doors.

They arrived as a very pregnant woman was unloading children from a limo. Paolo moved to greet the woman with an embrace and kiss, agreeing to her children's pleas to join them on the lawn after he said hello to his mother.

"This is not Isabella," the woman said with a significant look from Lauren to Paolo.

"No, this is Lauren Bradley," Paolo said, explaining to Lauren, "Maria is the second of my three sisters, all younger. She runs our branch in Switzerland. Her husband is with the Red Cross and must be overseas?" He looked to Maria.

"On his way back from that flood in Asia, which wasn't as horrific as feared, thankfully. It seems the earth-shattering events are happening at home today. What's going on, *caro fratello?*" Maria kept her tone artificially playful. "I thought the old Paolo had only been visiting three months ago. Has he returned to stay?"

Lauren heard the underlying hardness as clearly as Paolo did. He pulled away from the patronizing way Maria tried to thumb her lipstick off her brother's cheek. Lauren couldn't help but draw in on herself, assaulted by ignominy.

"Lauren is our guest, Maria. Don't make her feel uncomfortable. I don't like it." Paolo took Lauren's hand and pulled her into the house.

Lauren stumbled a little, feeling Maria's gaze like a dagger in her spine, but she was too terrified to look back and see what the woman was truly thinking. Apologies choked up her throat, but she couldn't voice them, not when Maria's reference to "the old Paolo" reminded Lauren of his promiscuous past and that she, Lauren, was merely his latest conquest.

A conquest full of consequences.

They moved purposefully through a classically

decorated house. It was more richly appointed than her mother's tasteful house where only company sat on the good furniture. People leaned and perched and nested everywhere, all talking a mile a minute, hands gesturing, all creating a din of cheerful Italian and bursts of laughter.

Lauren would have dug in her heels from being dragged into the crowd, but he rushed her past the startled eyes of his family.

She should have fought him on coming here today. She had thought she would be meeting his mother, not his entire family. She should have stayed at the house on the lake, should never have come to Italy. Why had she even called him when Ryan went missing? It had been a stupid, weak, desperate act.

Warm, stomach-grumbling scents greeted her when they entered the kitchen where copper pots steamed and marble workspaces were covered in trays and bowls. A woman with coiffed hair, perfect makeup, and not so much as a water stain on her apron turned from sending out a maid with a tray of hors d'oeuvres. Her smile for Paolo was warm and filled with love.

She checked slightly as she spotted Lauren.

"Mama, you remember Lauren." Paolo moved to embrace and kiss his mother. His wide shoulders eclipsed the confused astonishment on Carlotta Donatelli's face. By the time he had stepped back, she had recovered herself into the gracious woman Lauren had met at Ryan's funeral.

"Oh, my dear." Carlotta took up Lauren's hands. "Do you even remember me? What a difficult time for everyone. How are Elenore and Chris?"

"I haven't spoken to them recently," Lauren hedged, clearing her throat of a husk of culpability. "But, well, you saw them at the funeral. I don't imagine they'll ever recover."

The way I have. Lauren felt as though the baby in her belly glowed like a beacon of light, filling her with joy that must seem very inappropriate in these circumstances. The reality of being pregnant by this woman's son, a woman so close to Ryan's mother, hit Lauren. She began to really see how the underground tremor of their actions that one night would spread to topple and reshape the landscape around them. The Bradleys would be devastated all over again. This woman might side with them.

What would that do to Paolo? To his feelings for their child? For her?

Lauren dropped her gaze, growing more re-
morseful and devastated by the second. Her fingers went limp in Carlotta's delicate grip. She tried
telling herself the responsibility was split equally
between them, but family was family. The Donatellis would point their fingers toward Lauren as
the instigator. Whatever acrimony they directed
at Paolo would only be deflected by him onto the
woman who had caused him to be seen badly by
his family.

Strong hands gripped her shoulders and Paolo's
warm breath stirred the air near her cheek.

"Can I leave Lauren with you while I greet the
children, Mama? They're waiting for me."

Lauren turned her head in alarm, but he wasn't
looking at his mother as she half expected. He was
waiting for her gaze. He didn't glare in blame or
censure. He was conveying reassurance, letting her
know she shouldn't be nervous. At the same time,
his expression was one of such unabashed possessiveness, Lauren's heart flipped and her stomach swooped. Warmth flooded her and she was so
aware of his hard hands on her that when he slowly
released her, she felt a pang of loss.

She must look like the worst widow on earth,

blushing with sensual awareness and following Paolo's departure with puppy eyes.

If Carlotta judged her, she didn't let on. Her gaze followed her son, only coming back to Lauren when he was gone. By then her deep brown eyes were sharp with a mother's ability to sense without being told.

Had Paolo's significant stare been purely to plant a seed? Lauren wondered. She writhed inside, wanting that look to have been genuine, not a one-act play for his mother's sake.

With a reassuring smile, Carlotta said, "Can I ask you to put this bouquet in a vase while I stir these pots, Lauren? I rarely make the effort to cook anymore and now I remember why. I always get carried away and don't spend enough time with my guests. But if you'll keep me company, I won't feel left out. Tell me about yourself. I've always regretted not attending your wedding, but my husband had just passed. How did you and Ryan meet?"

Trembling inwardly, feeling on trial, Lauren went through the motions of trimming the ends of the flowers and arranging them in a vase while chatting with Carlotta. Paolo's mother was the niece of an Italian count and daughter of a diplomat, Lauren learned in return. Carlotta's excessively good breeding was in each of her eloquently-worded questions. None were so personal as to overstep, but she gently extracted what she wanted to know.

What had brought Lauren to Italy? Looking up family. Where was she staying? In a rented house out of the city. How long had she known Paolo? As long as she'd known Ryan.

If Carlotta had been anything but affably curious, Lauren might have been more cagey with her answers, but she found herself relaxing and wanting to confide as if they were longtime friends. It took all Lauren's concentration to keep from opening up more about her reasons for being here with Paolo today.

"I think his friendship with Ryan makes him feel responsible for me," Lauren hazarded as an excuse for her presence, heart panging at how true that was. Sexual desire aside, duty had brought him to Charleston and was the reason he had proposed.

She had to fight letting the corners of her mouth be tugged down by the thought.

"Paolo was devastated by Ryan's death. I'd never seen him like that except perhaps after my husband's death," Carlotta said with a pang.

Lauren left her nose in a freesia for a moment, thinking of how tortured Paolo had been in Charleston. That night hadn't been all sex. First Paolo had railed at God and war and his good friend while Lauren had silently wished she had been enough for Ryan so he would have been home with her and wouldn't have sent Paolo pacing and cursing and shaking his fists at the fates.

"He took Ryan's death very personally," she confided, needing to clear a catch from her throat. "He resents any kind of loss."

"You know him well." Carlotta cut her a swift, measuring look.

"I know his type," Lauren responded wryly.

Carlotta turned from stirring a rich, red sauce to cock her head at Lauren. "He and Ryan weren't as alike as most believe. They were both headstrong, high-energy boys, I'll admit, but Paolo was always testing himself, not us or our love. Elenore is my friend and I adore her, but Chris was hard on all of them. Paolo was driven by goals, but for Ryan, if his father said he couldn't, Ryan had to prove he could. He was like that with Paolo at times, straining Paolo's allegiance he was so stubbornly single-minded."

Like his determination to marry her when Lauren had said she was waiting for marriage. She hadn't been trying to manipulate him. Even Mamie had urged her, *Just have an affair, chou,* but Lauren had been such a good girl, so determined to keep her mother's love and approval, she had stuck by her price. Ryan had insisted on paying it rather than walk away. Because he was pigheaded? Or something else?

A thought flitted into Lauren's head. Had Ryan been trying to score a point against Paolo? Had he known Paolo was attracted to her and married her despite—perhaps even because of—Paolo's disapproval? She shook it off. Paolo hadn't known she and Ryan had stayed in touch after New York. She frowned.

"All right?" Carlotta prompted gently.

Lauren swallowed the scraped sensation at the back of her throat. "Just wondering why Ryan married me when he viewed settling down as giving up."

The words rang in the quiet room. Lauren took an appalled moment to absorb that she'd actually said them aloud. She couldn't imagine what Carlotta thought of her.

Carlotta only smiled tenderly beyond the window over the sink. "Paolo doesn't see it that way. He knows *bambinos* are an adventure in their own way. Look at him." She nodded at the glass.

Lauren felt a hitch of poignant anxiety as she moved to see Paolo holding up a swing so the occupant, Maria's daughter, was nose to nose with him. The girl's coloring and spirited grin gave the impression she could have been his daughter, not his niece. Whatever instructions she was imparting were making him nod very seriously until the conversation ended in a kiss on her forehead. He released her with a splay of his fingers, sending her sailing backward with a scream of delight. As she flew forward, he waited until the last second before he stepped back and lifted his hand above his head so she could aim for his fingertips with her toes.

Without thinking, Lauren let her hand settle on her abdomen where his blood, his genetics, his *bambino,* grew. Paolo would be an amazing father, she could see it. He would love his child in all the ways she dimly remembered her father had loved her.

If he ever acknowledged this baby as his.

Her heart invaded her throat, pulsing with a helpless ache. *She* knew the baby was his and he had already admitted he would come to care for the child even if he never believed it was. That was enough, wasn't it?

No, Lauren's heart cried.

"Paolo often takes on responsibility without being asked. I think that's what seeded his friendship with Ryan. He was trying to keep the American boy from killing himself with crazy stunts. I worry sometimes that he carries too much and doesn't know when to ask for help." Turning to face Lauren, Carlotta spoke with heart-stopping sobriety. "Much has been made of your staying with him in Charleston, but if you were there for him when he was hurting, I'm indebted to you."

She squeezed Lauren's forearm as she moved past her to the stove.

Lauren dropped her hand from her bellybutton, cringing as she feared how much she had revealed with her hand on her middle and the yearning in her eyes.

She knows.

Paolo glanced across to Lauren as they rose in the elevator to his penthouse, half expecting she was asleep on her feet, she was so quiet. Her head was pressed into the wall behind her and her lashes were heavy, but she blinked so her eyes were still open.

"Was the day too long for you?" he asked, realizing how late it was.

"I'm a bit talked out," she admitted, rolling her head toward him. A soft smile gave her a dreamy look that pulsed a measure of unexpected tenderness through him. "But your family is so fun. Maria apologized to me. Did you tell her to?"

"No, but I'm pleased that she did."

"It wasn't necessary. You might think she was meddling, but she only wants to protect you. I like her. I liked everyone."

"They liked you." He had enjoyed watching her charm his gregarious family with her quiet, genuine interest. She didn't always get the joke right away, but her Italian was good enough she got there eventually. The children had been fascinated by her stories of tapping maple syrup from the trees of her grandmother's estate and the old folks had speculated on which notorious rake could be her grandfather. She had fit in beautifully, filling him with pride at having her as his companion.

"You're lucky to have so many people care about you. You know that, don't you?" Her earnest eyes chided him against feeling any other way.

He nod-shrugged and braced the door for her as they arrived, keeping to himself that there were times when he questioned his luck. His biting conversation with Maria when he'd carried her sleeping toddler upstairs still grated.

I'm putting one and one together and coming up with three, she had leveled at him in an undertone, too sharp for anyone's good.

I've asked Lauren to marry me. I tell you that in confidence so you'll give her the respect she deserves, Paolo had returned implacably while his urgency to marry Lauren had increased. Pretending she was a friend visiting from Canada was annoying when his intentions were not only honorable, but something he was completely committed to.

Maria's head had snapped around with a searching expression. *Are you this time,* caro? *Confident?*

Paolo's guts had turned to water. He hadn't answered as indecision sat like a knot in his belly. He was aware of a growing desire that the baby be his. It scared him how badly he wanted that. Watching

Lauren play board games with the children and take every opportunity to hold his cousin's new baby had impressed on him that she was not only a woman who wanted to be a mother, but would take to the role naturally. The baby she carried was lucky and if the baby was his, *he* was lucky to have such a woman as mother to his offspring. Fear ate at him that he'd wind up devastated again while something deeper and fiercer demanded he claim her as his regardless.

Maria's watchfulness as he had processed all his emotions had been unbearable, reminding him she'd seen not just his humiliation of being cheated on in the past, but his heartache at losing out on being a father. He loathed bearing pity from his family. He was their rock, not the other way around.

It doesn't matter whose it is, he'd claimed to her. *She's the wife of my friend and needs a husband.* It had sounded a little too chivalrous even to him.

Maria had cautioned him not to act too hastily and he'd walked out on her accusing him of behaving impetuously out of grief.

That's not what this was. His feelings toward Ryan had become very contradictory. He harbored a lot of anger toward Ryan for the way he'd treated Lauren and, yes, Paolo couldn't help turning some of that responsibility on himself, but there was more to it. Ancient instincts of familial protectiveness were clamoring in him. He wanted Lauren in his cave, well buffered from predators or falls or starvation. He wanted her cub under his guardianship. It truly didn't matter to him whether the baby's DNA contained his so long as he could keep both of them.

He took a moment to absorb how comfortable he was with the notion of accepting another man's child. Because he knew it was unlikely he'd do so?

He worked his hands to dissipate the sweat that rose on his palms, disturbed by the path his mind was taking without any hard evidence. But it was tough to doubt Lauren when she was so lousy at subterfuge. More than a few lips had curled with conjecture when Lauren had declined wine, claiming, *Paolo said I could drive the Lambo if I stayed sober.*

He'd called her a dreamer and they'd shared a sparkling moment of rapport as she grinned cheekily at him. Her amusing remark had been a decent attempt at throwing people off the scent, but he couldn't escape the fact that since New York, she'd been speaking her mind very frankly to him.

He watched her balance against the sofa to remove her shoes and felt like he was the one who needed to brace himself as his view of Lauren tilted and realigned. She was careful about showing her feelings because she was sensitive, not manipulative. She put ailing old ladies and the reputation of an unfaithful husband ahead of her own needs. She did what felt right, not what was easy. Telling him about the baby hadn't been necessary. She could have left him to ride out the smudge on his reputation while rearing the baby alone. She had enough money—not his kind of money, but enough. She didn't need him or any man.

What if she'd chosen not to contact him? A frisson of fear took him in a delicate grip and squeezed.

"Do you mind if I go straight to bed?" Lauren covered a yawn then spoke from behind her hand when she noticed Paolo staring at her as though he'd never seen her before. "Is everything all right?"

"Your bag should be down here." He shuddered

slightly, as though pulling himself back from somewhere unpleasant.

Perhaps the day had been long for him, as well. He seemed pale and strained. In shock almost. Disturbed, Lauren chattered mindlessly as she followed him. "Dinners with my family are like a court proceeding. Growing up I always envied people like you. All I wanted was to be part of a family who loved each other like that."

He pressed open a door. "Now you can have it," he said with quiet but thunderous impact.

Lauren paused in the doorway, all but blind to the luxury of the guest suite and its decor of terra-cotta reds and mustard yellows. He had no idea how much she longed to be part of his family.

To hide her yearning, she wrinkled her nose and grinned at him with forced lightness. "Afraid the good looks, money and power aren't enough? You're throwing in your uncle's stories and your mother's ravioli? I *never* eat like that." She patted her middle as she moved into the room. "Where do you put it?"

He didn't say anything. She looked at him and his stare held a strange light that was nearly frightening in its intensity. She interpreted it as a demand for an answer.

"Don't think I'm not tempted." Lauren looked at fingers that knotted themselves together. "But saying yes makes everything real. I'll put that off as long as I can. It's been hard enough telling you and bearing your reaction." She couldn't help the edge of rebuke in her tone.

A flinch of compunction flashed across his face, leaving his brows knotted.

"I dread telling Mom," Lauren admitted. "Anyone else would be tickled to finally have a grandchild, but all she'll see is the timing. I should have been thinking about *her* that night in Charleston, you know, not myself," she said with a rasp of sarcasm. "She'll threaten to disown me."

In Charleston. Paolo's head went back as the words seemed to slap him. Lauren's bitter heartache was so uncouched and real. Helpless protectiveness ran through him. He didn't want to be the cause of a rift between her and her mother. He didn't want their child to be. It struck him that never once over the past few days had he felt *fear* of his family's reaction to her pregnancy.

Lauren didn't have that sense of acceptance. All

her little asides about her mother culminated in a picture that showed Paolo how much having this baby was costing her. Involving him made her situation infinitely more complicated, her troubles greater, not easier to bear.

Lauren had come to him for one reason only. He was the father of her baby and her personal ethics demanded she let him know that. Shame swamped him that he had rejected her word and resisted accepting his child for even one moment. At the same time, the reality of impending fatherhood suffused him in a mist of shocked numbness. He barely heard Lauren as she untied her scarf and continued speaking.

"When I found out I was pregnant, I actually considered telling her it was Ryan's. Pretend I went to a fertility clinic. She'd still hate me though."

"No," Paolo blurted out, appalled. He never should have left her vulnerable and coping alone for three months, nursing such desperate thoughts. He should have been with her from Charleston on.

"No, she wouldn't actually hate me," she agreed with a nervous glance at him for his vehemence. "But she'd act like she did. I can tell you right now, we could marry in her living room and she'd refuse to come to the wedding. She won't condone it."

"I mean, you can't tell her the baby is Ryan's." He was driven forward to grasp her arms. "This baby is mine."

His ferocity made her start a little and he unconsciously tightened his grip, staggered as the barriers he'd put up against accepting the baby fried into nothing. The truth was a surety in him. A terrifying excitement.

Lauren wore the same defenseless expression that probably contorted his own face. He hadn't expected it to be like this. He wasn't *choosing* to believe her. Certainty arrived with blunt force and it made him weak and invincible at the same time. He wasn't acknowledging facts in gentle ripples. Giant tsunami waves of conviction buffeted him, shifting the axis of his life, forging a new potency in him as he took on the emotional load that children were for any caring parent.

His life would never be the same.

"We didn't just make love that night. We made a baby." He grappled to absorb that a part of him was growing inside this woman, connecting them forever.

"I know," she returned, thick lashes blinking fast with shock over eyes that were growing shiny and tender. "I thought I told you that in New York."

His laugh caught as he pulled her close. Something tore open inside him. No misgivings behind it. Just joy tempered with pent-up prayers for his child's health and wellbeing. Tenderness for the woman in his arms, growing his child.

"I didn't want to believe you. I didn't want to be let down again," he choked out, beyond moved. Dizzy.

"I wouldn't do that to you." She drew back to set a warm hand on his jaw, her touch sincere, her beauty beyond physical. It radiated from her inner being.

The desire he always felt for her took a sharp turn into a swifter current of deeper waters. Kissing her wasn't a desire, it was a necessity. Gathering her into perfect alignment to his own body, he lowered his head to take her mouth with all the emotion flaring uncontrollably inside him.

Paolo's kiss was so sweet. Lauren moaned into it, afraid she would cry with joy. This was the reaction she hadn't dared dream of. He was kissing her like he loved her. She returned his ardor jubilantly, aware at the back of her mind that this could get out of hand fast, but that was okay. They were in complete accord now.

Their hands moved to reacquaint and she knew, oh she knew with a delicious clench of anticipation, that they were going to make love. He pressed his firm palm into her lower back and trailed his mouth down the side of her neck. She arched to offer herself, shivering when he grazed a sensitive spot. Her skin prickled with delight.

"Oh, Paolo." She clutched her fingers in his hair, feeling as though she'd shake apart she needed him so badly. She had *missed* him.

"I have to touch you, Lauren. I love the way you feel."

Her heart tripped as he spoke the *l*-word. The voice in the back of her mind waved another caution flag, but she ignored it. Her world had been absent of his life-giving caresses for too long.

He lifted his head and the hunger in his gaze nearly swallowed her whole. Her stomach dipped while a powerful zing of pure need struck that delicious spot where she was mashed against his fervent heat. Because it was him and he seemed to bring it out in her, she let instinct guide her and tilted her hips, seeking more pressure and a better, more acutely sensitive angle.

He growled something in Italian, but she drew him down to kiss her again while carefully backing toward the bed. He never stopped kissing her, the movement of his mouth wickedly hard in its power, tongue invading to pleasure and possess, as though he was trying to anchor her to him while she insistently drew him along as she flowed backward.

She melted onto the bed, pulling him onto her like a weighted blanket, squirming deliciously as he settled half over her.

He used his thigh as a weight to control her restless legs, almost as if he was trying to keep this from going too far too fast, but she was determined to let the wildness take them both. She longed to feel him losing control the way he had that night in Charleston. Her deepest, darkest needs had been met when he'd been as desperate for her as she'd been for him. It couldn't happen fast enough for her.

She cupped his head and did her best to incite him, urging him to settle completely on her. When he kept his weight on his elbow, she used the space to arch and reach the zip of her dress.

Paolo helped her, but didn't pull her sleeve down her shoulder, just cupped her breast through the loosened fabric and gently massaged, slowly driving her crazy. Her nipple ached for proper attention and she whimpered, covering his hand, conveying that she needed more pressure. He lightly bit at the nipple through the dress and she encouraged him with a whispered plea.

He groaned out another spate of Italian, something about trying to kill him, and kissed her with sudden raw passion, scattering her thoughts so she knew nothing but the heat of his leg on hers and the much anticipated stroke of his hand from her rib cage down past her hip, under her dress, up her thigh and then—

She raked her fingertips down his back then pulled his shirt free and sought the hot skin of his back. Her entire being went taut with expectancy, tingling under his trace of her underpants. With a small lift of her hips she encouraged him and he rewarded her by sliding his fingers beneath the lace. His knowing touch parted and pressed and slowly caressed as he gently worked his hand into intimate contact with her wet center.

She rocked her hips, hands moving mindlessly

on his flexing back as she set the pace. He complied with her signals, lovingly stroking her into madness.

When the sweetness grew too sharp to bear, Lauren dug her nails into his spine. She tried to escape the pressure of his kiss to tell him. She wanted to strip and feel him push his thick penis inside her, but he used his stronger body and all-encompassing kiss to keep her exactly where she was, at the mercy of his unrelenting touch. He refused to let up on the lazy stroking and the cataclysm engulfed her before she could stop it, tumbling through her in an avalanche of thunderous pulses, sending quakes of pleasure echoing through her that were so deep she bit back a scream at the intensity of it.

Slowly she came back to herself. Paolo was kissing her very tenderly between her panting breaths. He extricated his hand from beneath her skirt and she tried to roll into him, sensitized to everything about him: the extreme tension gripping him, the erection thrusting imperiously against her thigh, the blood pounding hard in his throat as she moved her hands to cradle his jaw and tried to bring his mouth to hers.

"Tesoro," he murmured, roaming his lips over her face. "You have to marry me. You know that, *si?"*

Delicious lassitude gripped her, but so did a desire to bring him the same pleasure he'd just given her. Marry and do this for the rest of their lives?

"Yes, of course," she breathed. Her head felt heavy as she lifted to touch her lips to his and only grazed his chin.

He pulled away even further, lightly brushing off her touch while his gaze skimmed down her body, gleaming with ardent possessiveness. Flicking her dress down to cover her thighs, he levered from the bed.

"Where are you going?" She didn't mean to sound so desperate, but she didn't understand. Protection wasn't an issue—

"To make the arrangements," he answered, his smile tight. "Tempted as I am, I said I'd wait until we're married. I will."

He walked out.

CHAPTER NINE

LAUREN DIDN'T SLEEP. She didn't cry, either, even though her eyes burned. She stayed on the bed fully clothed, curled around her aching stomach where fury burned in its pit. He was such a *man*.

Perhaps not a typical one. She wasn't a complete idiot about biology and the battle of the sexes. She knew women were usually the ones left unfulfilled while their partners snored off their climaxes. Not that Ryan had ever left her frustrated sexually. He'd always taken the attitude that if she wasn't finished, he wasn't finished. At first she'd viewed his attention to detail as proof that he was enamored with her. Later she realized it was more to do with his drive to conquer women through seduction. It had made her sick to realize she was just one more scratch in his headboard.

She felt sick now.

For all his talk about chemistry, Paolo wasn't nearly as affected by her as she was by him. That made her want to pull back in and disappear. She thought about checking train schedules, but running away was so cowardly. So *virginal*. And she'd promised to marry him. That wasn't just a promise, but something she knew in her heart was best for their baby. All her reasons stood strong. Except that she'd let herself believe for ten minutes that Paolo cared for her and had found out she'd been right in the first place. She meant nothing to him.

Her ego withered as she remembered how quickly she'd become besotted. She had let herself read into his sudden show of emotion that, she realized now, had been for the baby growing inside her. *I love the way you feel.* His thumb and forefinger had been spanning from hipbone to hipbone across her navel when he'd said it, but she'd made it about her.

She tried telling herself that marrying knowing full well that his feelings were only physical was okay, but that was the crux of it. Not that she'd climbed the hill of hope and had a tumble. No, she had thought they were evenly matched in the lust department and they weren't. She'd just made all the advances—again!—while he had been undeniably aroused but had walked away.

To make *arrangements*.

Oh, hell no.

Paolo frowned as he removed his nona's ring from his safe, determined to give it to Lauren, but briefly wondering if she would accept it. Of course she would. She had agreed to marry him, but the ring had been in the family several generations. It was so old, the diamond's shape was slightly imperfect because it had been cut by hand long before the precision of modern techniques. Would she see that as quaint or substandard? Perhaps rather than an engagement ring, it should be a wedding present.

Dio! His hand was shaking, his body was so wildly keyed-up with sexual tension.

He was proud of himself though. He'd sworn to marry Lauren before he made love to her again and he would, even though the way she had burst into flames at his touch had nearly taken him apart at the seams. Leaving her when she'd been pliant and aroused had nearly killed him. Only his determination to marry her first had kept him from taking her.

Not that anyone appreciated the level of control he was showing. Everyone he'd just spoken to, right down to his mother and her surprised pause when he'd informed her of the private ceremony he and Lauren would have in the archbishop's office tomorrow, had suggested he was acting rashly.

They were all wrong. The baby was his. A prompt marriage was imperative.

It was also convenient that rushing the ceremony would allow him to keep his vow without suffering too long. His need for her was acute.

His laptop gave a muted blip signaling one of the emails he'd requested had arrived. He turned to find Lauren standing in the doorway of his office. Her chic dress had been replaced with a pair of baggy pajama pants and a waffle-weave shirt with sleeves chopped off at the elbows. Her face was clean of makeup, her expression strained and stiff.

Her gaze held his for the barest fraction of a second before averting to a safe place beyond his shoulder while her chin thrust out defensively. Her body language hardened into unreceptive lines.

He had a sudden and disturbing flashback to their Morning After in Charleston. She'd been exactly like this after waking up with blatant mortification beside him. He remembered very clearly the way their naked limbs had been tangled and lax. One or the other had shifted in sleep, stirring both of them. Paolo had unconsciously tightened his arms around her, involuntarily growing hard as awareness of who was next to him and memories of their night had rushed in. They had opened their eyes nose to nose with each other.

Despite the compunction that had slammed through him, waking with her soft skin brushing against his nudity had been wonderful. The horror that had paled her face had quickly dampened his gratification however.

Until now, he had refused to go back to that morning. He'd been filled with self-recrimination that had sprung from abandoning his self-discipline and betraying his friend. He'd sensed, however, that Lauren's regret ran to something deeper and more profound, as though she had been ashamed to have shared herself with him. Her hurry to push away from him had been almost panicked, her desperate silence suggesting she wanted to wipe out the entire experience.

He had rolled away when she had, numbing the bite of rejection with self-disgust. Reproach had saved him, allowing him to blame her for their transgression. He had labeled the havoc inside him "guilt" and used it to harden himself against her. She had distanced herself physically and emotionally, surrounding herself with gate-keeping mourners while he had attached ulterior motives to her actions so he could form a line of contempt between them.

He hadn't liked how vulnerable Lauren had made him feel. He still didn't. He'd managed to control himself this evening, but that balm to his ego didn't go very far. The baby was his, the marriage in process, but uneasiness loomed like a storm.

Sexual tension, he dismissed. It had been months since their tryst and after this evening, his control was hanging by a thread. If he felt edgy, it was at his ability to continue resisting her. Once they were married and he didn't have to, this nameless agitation would disappear.

His strain to hold himself tightly-reined showed as he gruffly offered her the ring. "It was my nona's. She was still alive the first time I married. My ex never wore it. I'd like you to."

Lauren curled her hands into fists of refusal and tucked them under her arms.

His heart took that like a knife. He set the ring

on his desk, masking the sting of having the heir-loom snubbed. "Of course, if you'd prefer something more modern—"

"I'd prefer," she said icily, "if you didn't treat me like a damned sex toy to be picked up and set aside when it suits you! I'm not like you, you know. Making love means something to me."

As opening volleys went, it detonated like a percussion grenade, leaving his inner ears vibrating. "You think walking away from you was easy?" He was instantly at the same level of anger she was projecting, still riding a wave of intense sexual frustration.

"Oh, I could tell it was hard, Paolo," she seethed. "But your silly bet was more important to you than what was going on between us. Do you have any idea how that makes me feel?"

Part of Lauren was screaming in horror that she was revealing herself this way, urging her to clam up and brush this whole thing under the rug. The other part couldn't stay silent. She was too angry.

"Pitiful," she supplied. "I'm not proud that I lack inhibition around you, but at least when I let go in Charleston you were there with me. Tonight you sure weren't! I hate that you can control this attraction between us and I can't. If you think I'm going to marry into an imbalance like that, you're crazy."

Her rejection of marriage seemed to make him stand taller while he narrowed his eyes to keen slits. "Is that why you acted like I had contaminated you the morning after in Charleston? You were embarrassed by how abandoned you'd been?"

Lauren swallowed, regretting calling attention to how unconstrained she'd been. A blush rose to swallow her face in a rancid burn. She ignored it to mutter, "When Ryan and I—"

"Never talk to me about the two of you in bed together," Paolo snarled, cutting his hand through the air to mentally slam shut a door he would never open. Ever. He could barely stand knowing it had happened. He wouldn't listen to the details.

Lauren swayed as though buffeted by the force of his antagonism.

He looked away, not willing to apologize for his outburst, but dismayed that he was revealing how sensitive he was to the topic.

"—married," she finished with a tremor of incredulity. "I was only saying that when we got married, I'd never even kissed another man. That sort of inexperience was always a disadvantage. You've had a million lovers and—"

"None of those women meant to me what Ryan meant to you," he ground out. "Do you think you're the only one worrying about comparisons?"

The question stunned her. Her hands went clammy and her mind went blank.

He gathered himself into a haughty cloud of resentful humility. "Why do you think I tried to stop you that night in Charleston?" he growled. "I thought you were reaching for him. I won't be his stand-in."

Her mouth opened, but whatever words she might have found caught in her throat. She had never seen Paolo anything but aristocratic and arrogant and entitled, but right now his pride lay on the floor between them as clearly as a skinned hide. She had to tread very carefully.

He rubbed his face. "*Dio!* Perhaps we should be ashamed of ourselves for falling into bed that night without considering who it could hurt, but what we did there…don't be ashamed of that, Lauren. I tried to tell you once before, I like that you respond to me as strongly as I respond to you."

Then why did you walk away tonight? she wanted

to shout, while the rest of what he'd said set a lump of emotion into her throat. "Ryan wasn't home enough for me to take for granted he would be in my bed. Of course I knew it was you." That's *why* she had reached for him. It had been the culmination of a thousand repressed fantasies.

"And I knew it was you," Paolo stated forcefully. "You're not some meaningless hookup, Lauren."

She searched his closed expression, yearning to believe he was telling the truth, but it seemed so implausible. She was a boring, small-town goody-goody.

Paolo could barely breathe. His lungs felt as though they were being sawed in two while guilt and other emotions tried to smother him. Lauren was pushing him into a territory of self-examination where he didn't want to go. Yes, there had been a lot of women. Yes, it was true that making love with them had never been an act of making *love*. He had never seen anything shameful in it because the women he'd been with had all been looking for what he also wanted: physical release.

Suddenly he was deeply ashamed though. His very active, if well-protected sex life was sordid when held up to her *making love means something to me.*

But that was another way of saying that Ryan had meant something to her. He hated knowing that she might be angry with her dead husband, but still had feelings for him.

Sex always demanded emotion from a woman, though. Paolo knew that. They put their small frames at the mercy of a much stronger being. That required a level of trust men didn't need. Men weren't vulnerable when they stripped and covered a woman. They were indomitable. That's why they liked sex so much.

With Lauren, everything was different. Paolo's inner warrior became defenseless, making him balk at revealing any signs of weakness, but he'd dented her self-confidence tonight. That demanded that he set aside his shields and make things right.

"You want me to say that making love to you was more important than marrying you first, but I can't," he admitted gruffly, facing a demon he hadn't fully confronted until now, when he couldn't avoid it. "I need you to have my name. I won't have Mrs. Bradley in my bed again."

Her jaw slacked and her face paled to white before outraged color flooded in. "That's disgusting!"

He rushed her, taking her arms. "I'm not proud of this jealousy," he bit out. "But we're being honest here."

"Jea—" She stilled her struggle and lifted her gaze to his, wary. "It's not just a competition thing?"

"What? No! He's not even here to see that you're mine now."

"Exactly. He's not here, so how could you feel jealous of a name that I'm not even using?"

Dio! Her naïveté astonished him.

"I've *always* been jealous," he elaborated.

Lauren's fingernails hurt. She realized distantly that she had her fists knotted in Paolo's shirt, her grasp so hard her nails were bending, but even while tension held her in its silent grip, deep inside she unfurled a bit. If he was being honest...

"I don't have any right to it," Paolo allowed begrudgingly, "but from the moment he slid into our booth and you barely looked at me again, I have been eaten up with it."

Lauren forced herself to release him, unnerved by what he was saying. Logically she knew there was nothing particularly reassuring about a man revealing his territorial streak. Jealousy was a sign of distrust, not love, but a nebulous hope tried to take root in her breastbone, painful in its worming to take hold. It seemed like a start.

"Did he know?"

"What do you think?" he retorted flatly, letting his hands drop away from her to find his pockets.

The moments following their kiss at the wedding came back to her, both men crackling with territorial aggression. And then there was that conversation she and Ryan had had in the bridal suite later on, when he'd casually revealed that Paolo had tried to talk him out of going through with the wedding. She'd interpreted it as Paolo trying to save his friend from a woman he deemed unworthy, but now it took on a different connotation as did the way Ryan had watched her so closely as he relayed it.

"Do you..." She rubbed her forehead, trying to ease the tension there. "Do you think he married me just to hurt you?"

Lauren's question notched higher the suspicion Paolo had been holding off with bone-gripping denial. It wasn't just the treachery it implied. It was a blow to a woman who was already struggling to recover from infidelity. To learn her husband had never really loved her was too cruel to suggest.

For long seconds he refused to look at her, but was ultimately unable to lie to her. When he finally did take in her anxious pallor, regret cut through him like a broadsword. He had never, ever meant to draw her into what he now feared had always been more feud than friendship.

"He had his own jealousies," he allowed, holding out a hand that she ignored. "You know what his father was like. Mine was proud and supportive… In Ryan's eyes I was spoiled, living an easy life."

"So it's possible." Her voice sounded like she'd swallowed broken glass.

"At the time I thought he was marrying you because you made him happy." It was easy enough to believe when he'd coveted her for himself. "If I'd suspected otherwise, I really would have stopped it."

She shrugged that off, lost in a place that pulled down the corners of her mouth.

"Look at me." Taking a firm grip of her soft chin, he waited for her shattered gaze to tentatively meet his.

He gentled his touch so he was caressing her downy skin, trying to ease the anguish from her expression while a personal hurt reared inside him. "You walked away from me and went to him more than once. I thought he made you happy, too. That was important to me, that you were happy."

Her lips quivered and he stilled them with the brush of his thumb.

"I thought you wanted nothing to do with me," he admitted gruffly. "That's why it meant everything when you knew it was me you were making love to that night in Charleston." The floor became quicksand beneath him as he opened himself up this way.

Her breath hitched and her yellow-brown eyes melted into liquid gold. "You realize my passport says Lauren Green."

Paolo's body seemed to consolidate into a statue of tested strength. His grip hardened on her chin. His eyes closed and for long seconds his only movement was the flare of his nostrils and the visible pound of his pulse in his throat.

"You are a cruel, cruel woman, Ms. Green."

She couldn't help the wicked smile that traced

itself across her lips. Her heart fluttered in pleasure and anticipation.

He looked down at her with pupils that had expanded to swallow all the color from his irises, inciting a shiver of delicious excitement. His hand slid to her neck and his other one splayed at her waist, firm and possessive.

"But this is important to me, Lauren. I want my wife in my bed. No one else."

Lauren was still anxious at how fast things were moving between them, but honestly, if she had wanted to raise this baby alone, she never should have told Paolo he was the father. He was too paternal to let that go and she wanted him in her life.

Her heart gave a little *thunk* as she realized she might have been expressing that desire with her phone call to him. As foreboding as Ryan's disappearance had been, she hadn't been reacting as a wife fearing for her husband. Her marriage had been over. Ryan had been a big part of her life and she would never want him to suffer the kind of tragic end he'd met, but she could have waited to hear the truth. She had known answers would come eventually, delivered on the standard military need-to-know basis.

Instead she'd seized the excuse to reach out to Paolo, sensing that her tenuous connection to him was about to fray away completely. The truth was, she had been longing for five years to explore what might have happened between them if Paolo had not been engaged when they had met in New York.

Her heart felt like it was beating outside her body, unprotected and at risk. The reason she had turned to Ryan in the first place was that he hadn't been able to reach through her inner barriers the way Paolo did. That spinelessness had led her to marry the wrong man.

As scary as it was to open herself to Paolo, she had to or they'd never stand a chance. There was no shrinking back into the shadows here. She'd come too far. It was time to adapt to the new world she'd put herself in.

She nodded jerkily. "I want to be married, too."

Until she saw the ease that washed over him, she hadn't realized how tense he'd been. Marrying her *was* important to him. Touched, she let her gaze flick to the desk where he'd left the ring.

He stepped back, hands dropping away from her. "If you don't like it—"

"What? No! I didn't mean to be rude about it.

I was just so angry— Oh, Paolo, it's lovely." She melted into near tears as she took a proper look at the antique ring, so simple and delicate and obviously treasured.

He slid the ring onto her finger and lifted her hand to kiss her knuckles, his expression shining with masculine pride.

And from there they had to have a real kiss. Had to. He moved his hand to the back of her neck, holding her in place while he stole one deep kiss after another, his mouth moving on hers as though savoring her. Lauren moaned in pleasure, but before she could press herself into the hard ridge of his erection, he pressed her back in a show of merciless discipline.

"Get some sleep," he said gruffly. "Because I swear after that ceremony tomorrow, I'll be keeping you awake. A lot."

CHAPTER TEN

SOMEHOW PAOLO PROCURED a perfect wedding dress overnight. The simple sheath with an overlay of eggshell lace was stylishly understated, just right for a midmorning wedding. New shoes, better than Cinderella's, were a perfect fit and sparkled with promise. Her hat with a short veil completed the outfit, making her feel chic and sophisticated.

All good omens, Lauren told herself, as her groom's appearance nearly knocked her off her feet.

The familiar couched energy of Paolo's dynamic personality was vaguely austere in a tailored Italian suit. His shoulders, sharply defined by the cut of his jacket, eased slightly when he saw her. He looked a little tired, a lot determined, and sexy as hell.

Nerves struck her. Marriage was permanent. Not to be entered into lightly. At the same time, Lauren had the sentient feeling that this was inevitable. Like she and Paolo would have come to this no matter what.

Therefore, it seemed both right and surreal that he took her to a towering cathedral to speak their vows before an archbishop, of all people. Paolo had said it would be a small, private ceremony with only two witnesses, so she wasn't entirely surprised to see Vittorio and Maria waiting on the steps, Maria's daughter Alys in tow.

"Don't be nervous," Maria urged Lauren when she realized how intimidated Lauren was. "He's a family friend. He marries all of us and would be insulted if Paolo hadn't asked him. Although he's a little put out with the speed. I can't imagine what Paolo paid him to waive the banns. When my brother makes up his mind, though, don't even think of getting in his way."

"Is this a *wedding?*" Alys nearly leapt out of her skin. "When Mama said to wear my church dress, I thought it was for mass."

Paolo reached a hand to Alys's curly head. "Didn't you make me promise that when I married, you could be my flower girl? Vittorio brought bouquets and everything."

Vittorio greeted Lauren with a lazy kiss on her

cheek, looking slightly hungover and unabashedly amused as he handed over the flowers.

Alys grasped her posy in reverent hands, her adoring eyes lifting to Paolo. "Oh, Uncle, I *love* you."

They all laughed, but Lauren grew teary-eyed at the same time. Of course Alys loved him. Who could resist a man who kept promises to little girls? Whether he kept promises to big ones, was the question.

She was distracted from her fears as they entered the reverent building and she was introduced to the archbishop. The ceremony was under way seconds later.

And it was too easy. Lauren had done the fairy-tale thing with Ryan, working herself into knots over every small detail of the huge event, agonizing through the ceremony with so many eyes upon her while her own focus kept slipping to the brooding man on Ryan's right.

This was intimate and solemn and very much between the two of them. Which made it almost too big for Lauren to handle. She was hypersensitive to his concerned frown as he took her cold hands in his warm ones and massaged lightly to warm them. She began to well up as Paolo looked into her eyes to make his vows. It was too impactful. *Lack of sleep,* she tried telling herself, but her throat was one big lump of hope that he meant these vows. By the time he kissed her, she was trembling with the effort not to reveal how susceptible to him she was.

He wrapped his strong arms around her and drew her in, promising to square up all her loose edges with one warm, comforting embrace.

"Are you okay?" he murmured.

She wasn't. Everything about this was too right, leaving her deeply disturbed by how skinless he felt. She hid her expression by tilting her head down.

"It's just the baby making me emotional," she whispered in excuse, and felt a tender kiss brush her temple.

They broke apart as Maria announced she had to get back to the rest of her children. "Are you coming to the house?" she asked Paolo.

"I've already made my apologies to Mama. I promised Lauren I'd take her south for our honeymoon. We'll be back in a week."

They were in the air to Sicily within thirty minutes. Something must have shown on Lauren's face as she returned to her seat after changing in the very well-appointed bedroom on the private jet because Paolo gave her a laconic grin before rising to take his turn. "I don't want to be interrupted and we'd have to take our seats to land."

Oh. She was that obvious, was she? It took everything she had to act naturally as they ate a light lunch. Every cell of her being was locked on him, filling the air around them with an aura of sexual tension.

Once they landed, Paolo murmured something about her desire to see his country as he instructed their driver to take them on the coastal route from Catania to Taormina. The scenery was pretty enough, offering glimpses of clear blue waves lapping at stretches of sand and rocky escarpments interspersed with pockets of village life and tourist havens. Lauren appreciated his thoughtfulness, but she was ever aware of the silent man beside her, seemingly gripped in a similar stasis of impatience.

They climbed something the driver called Monte Tauro. The road entered a charming village high off the water and the grandness of the position and view of snowcapped Mount Etna prompted a wonder-filled "Oh" of reaction out of her. They passed a tram making a steep decline to the water and she craned her neck.

"It saves hiking down to the beach. The water is warm year round. We could swim if you'd like," he said.

"You expect we'll leave the villa?" she joked, her nerves strained to screaming pitch by the suppressed desire crackling between them.

Paolo laughed with rich appreciation and crushed her hand in his, fingers weaving between hers in a determined grip of possession. The car stopped and he pulled her out behind him into a sunny courtyard where bougainvillea bloomed in bursts of red on spidery green tendrils clinging to the stone walls of the house.

He dismissed the staff and brought the luggage in himself while Lauren moved through the lavish interior of the small home. Outside, the deck of the infinity pool seemed to drop into the horizon and she wedged herself into a corner of the terrace next to it, seeking the warmth of slanting sunshine as she savored the simmering sensuality inside her. Heat gathered in the stainless steel rail and each breath she took was a sexy inhale of anticipation.

"Are you hungry?"

Paolo's graveled voice abraded her taut nerves. Suppressing a little shiver, Lauren shook her head, then quarter-turned to look at him.

The sun was in her eyes and he was in shadow. All she saw was the silhouette of his razor-sharp business pants and the way his muscles strained his shirt. Glints of light in her periphery, possibly reflections off the neighbor's pool below, gilded his figure and threw his frame into a relief map of powerful male beauty.

Flutters of feminine response started in her abdomen. She involuntarily tensed against them, gripping the rail tighter as she saw the tornado forming and knew she couldn't escape it. As her pupils adjusted, she received an impression of blazing eyes and a face lined with lust.

"Come here," he growled.

Lauren gave a tiny shudder as though he'd shouted when his voice was only raspy with desire. At the same time, the glint in her eyes seemed to become more deliberate.

She raised a hand to shield her vision and glanced

below. "I think there's someone down there with binoculars."

Paolo crowded into the small space next to her, nearly frying her mind, but the flash of a lens fixed on them like a laser pointer from one of the properties below.

"It's fine," he said, settling his hands on her waist to lightly force her into turning to face him. As her body brushed his, need flared inside her. It was all she could do to steel herself against him as her fingers draped his biceps in subtle resistance.

"But it could be paparazzi. Mom and the Bradleys don't even know—"

"I called them last night," he told her. "We needed declarations that there were no impediments to our marrying. Given your reservations about talking to your mother, I took the liberty."

"You what!" She pressed back into the rail behind her.

"I asked her if we should wait until she was available to attend the wedding or make it official immediately. I realize that's a clichéd negotiating tactic, giving her a choice between yes and yes, but it worked. She supports the marriage," he said dryly.

Nevertheless, Gabrielle Reid had registered her disapproval. Lauren could sense it in the way Paolo took on a look of suppressed umbrage.

"Yes, well, marrying was the right thing to do," Lauren said into the middle of his chest, both relieved and dreading her next call home. She quickly asked, "And Elenore?"

She braced herself, too often the target of judgment from Ryan's mother to take her reaction lightly.

"Chris made a declaration on your behalf." A muscle pulsed in Paolo's jaw. "He wasn't happy, but it's done. Everyone liable to be affected is aware that we've married. This photographer works for a friend." He nodded to the camera below. "They'll leak the news with the least amount of sensationalism. No more secrets, no more impediments."

A rush of power and excitement surged in him as he absorbed their freedom to finally be together. The feeling had its root in sexual anticipation but carried subtle branches of pride and triumph and elation. She was his now. His hands tightened on her.

"He'll leave us alone shortly," he assured her. "Meantime, let's give him what he's being paid for."

Lauren ducked his kiss before it landed, skittering her gaze toward the pool next to their feet, her only direction of escape.

Paolo frowned. "What's wrong?"

"I don't want to play the devoted wife for the world again," she said, flickering a glance of hurt up at him. "This is between you and me, Paolo. It's real and it's private."

He was oddly touched, realizing that Lauren wasn't just being shy. When something meant a lot to you, you protected it. Her sensitivity to intrusion spoke volumes about how important their intimacy was to her.

"You're right. Come, *Signora Donatelli*. I've waited too long to have you to myself." Taking her hand, he led her into the villa.

The ivory walls and linens in the bedroom reflected the rosy glow of the sinking sun. Lauren's heels made a soft click on the marble as they moved into the cavernous room. She unconsciously tightened her hand on his to prevent a slip.

Paolo took it as a signal to stop and turned to face her. His hands came up to the buttons of her shirt.

Lauren drew back in surprise at his forwardness.

A smile twitched his lips. "I'm not rushing you, just dying to see how the baby is changing you..." He tugged the tails of her shirt free while Lauren bit her lip, unable to keep from grinning as he parted the edges of her blouse and looked down.

"There's hardly anything there, but I'm ridiculously proud," she confided, holding her shirt parted as Paolo unbuttoned her pants and lowered the zip.

His warm hands rolled back her fly to expose the pale swell of her abdomen, the subtle shape only discernible because she was naturally slender. He let his hands rest at her bare waist for a few moments, forehead tilted against hers. She could see a doting smile playing over his lips.

Fascinated, Lauren reached to trace the shape with her finger, seduced by their smooth texture.

He caught her hand and kissed her palm. "I'm glad you're having my baby, *la mia adorata*."

His quiet ferocity sent a cupid's arrow of sweet joy through her. "Me, too," she said in a voice thinned by deep emotion.

"I'm also intrigued by the lack of a bra." His darkening eyes lowered to gaze on her chest as he lightly brushed the shirt back on her shoulders, exposing her bare breasts.

Stimulated by the tickling brush of fabric and his caressing touch, Lauren stood straighter and sucked in a startled breath, unconsciously lifting her breasts into prominence. The combination of cool air and hot focus from Paolo's avid gaze made the orbs go tight, the nipples pinching sharply, contracting into thrusting points.

"All my bras got too small overnight," she confided, losing her train of thought and shakily gasping for air as he traced the outsides of her breasts with light fingertips. The heaviness in her breasts increased. They seemed to fill and harden, nearly painful in their sensitivity to his light, light touch.

"Hurray for growing out of bras." He came a half step closer and very, very gently enveloped her breasts in his hot hands, slowly closing them in firm cups that made her blood thicken into the soles of her feet.

She whimpered at the sensation of swirling pleasure spiraling from her middle into the hot ache between her thighs. His grip loosened. "Too much?"

She couldn't speak, could only clutch at him as she swayed on her feet.

"You're so beautiful, Lauren." His hot breath caressed her neck while he slid his hands into her pants to begin easing them down her bottom.

She couldn't help wriggling her cheeks into his sure hands.

He paused long enough to groan with approval and say, "I'm trying to hang on to control here, *cara.* Help me out."

"I like it when you lose control," she said, then bit her lips together.

He flashed her a look that was a little incredulous, a little wary, and very, very dangerous. A muscle pulsed in his jaw as he lowered to squat before her, drawing her pants down her legs without any increased urgency, but a fresh, very thick sexual tension imbuing his movements.

"We're going to keep these on for a minute," he said as he threaded her pants over her shoes, one hand steady on her hip to keep her balanced. "Because there's something I need to tell you." He threw her pants away and gazed at her nude limbs. The angle of her high heels contracted the lithe muscles of her thighs and calves, elongating her legs and making her feel strong even though she was nearly shaking with nervous arousal.

"What?" Lauren prompted, voice a husky whisper deep in her throat.

"I." He made her wait as he wound his gaze down to her polished toenails. One finger traced the cheeky strap around her ankle, then his gaze climbed up her shin and knee to the length of her thigh where he stared a long time. "Am a leg man. And yours are exquisite." He followed the path with his hands, drifting his caressing touch up sensitive skin and twitching calves, smoothing the backs of her thighs to her backside so his long fingers teased the sensitive globes of her bottom through the silk of her underpants.

Lauren's stomach flip-flopped, making her exhale through a tickling sensation that was in her nerves and muscles and blood. Wild sensations made her legs quiver and she shifted self-consciously.

Paolo slid one hand down to her ankle. "I have been stealing looks for years, *cucciola mia.* Today I can look and touch and kiss…" His knowing fingers found the sensitive skin at the back of her knee, making her reflexively shift her weight and retract her leg.

His strong grip at her hip kept her steady on one

shoe while he bent her knee and brought her inner thigh to his mouth so he could nuzzle his hot, firm lips against her skin, grazing damp kisses that incited her to mewl in distress.

"I won't let you fall," he murmured reassuringly, shoulder muscles flexing under her grasping hands as she tried to balance.

"It's not that. I—" Lauren swallowed, dizzy and a little frantic. Her fingers dived into his hair to stop what he was doing to her and when she had both feet on the ground she instinctively pressed her thighs together, trying to ease the throbbing pulse between them.

Paolo chuckled softly, his breath on the lace triangle a sinful caress. He hooked his finger in them and tugged one side down.

With Paolo's sultry eyes holding hers in a kind of trance, Lauren let her thighs relax so he could drag the scrap of lace and silk down to her knees.

They dropped around her ankles and he sat back on his heels for a long, unabashed study.

"Step out of them." It was a graveled command, but his knuckles showed white where his hands rested on his thighs. The rise and fall of his chest was uneven.

Seduced by how affected he was, she brazenly lifted one foot then the other, setting her feet down well on either side of the abandoned lace.

Paolo's breath hissed in and he lifted his gaze in an agonizingly slow and sensual drift upward, making each square inch of her tremble and burn. Her thighs shivered, the secretive place between dampened with liquid heat, pulsing for the breach of his thick shaft. Her stomach quivered under the impact of his gaze and her breasts thrust upward again, this time in proud invitation as she took a constricted breath.

Like an animal scenting his mate, his nostrils flared and he rose in a rush of power, overwhelming her in a heartbeat with his looming size. But his grip was gentle as he pulled her into him, crushing her naked front into his clothed one while he took her mouth in a rapacious kiss.

They both opened their lips in passionate hunger. The flick of his tongue was a claiming and they were pulled into the undertow of suppressed desire released at last.

Every blood vessel in her body lit up where she pressed to him, like polarity on a magnet gravitating to its source of attraction. Her skin flooded with sensitivity and she couldn't help rubbing the aching orbs of her breasts into the friction of his shirt. The tips stung with need.

Paolo made a noise in his throat that was pure, frustrated predator. She understood. He was roaming his hands over her, melding her to him as though he could absorb her through his skin. She couldn't reach enough of him, but his clothes were in the way. Both wanted the offending garments gone and neither wanted to pull away to remove them.

Lauren tilted her hips, intuitively seeking contact with the hard proof of his craving for her. She lifted higher on her tiptoes at the same time. Her fingers dug through his hair and she pulled him down as she pressed her lips harder to his, yearning for everything he could give her. Now. *Please.*

With a curse, he dragged his head up and pressed her back a step.

She couldn't help it. A hitch of horror and chagrin caught her. It was last night all over again.

"*Dio!* Don't look at me like that! You're pregnant. I'm not going to take you to the damned floor. I'm about to—"

Before she realized what he was doing, he had

swooped low and caught his arm behind her knees, sweeping her into a cradle against his chest. His long legs took the few steps to the bed and he set her there gently, glaring with disgruntlement.

"One of us has to try to control this."

Lauren didn't move, too fascinated by the struggle she could see behind his scowl. His skin was dark with a flush of arousal, his movements jerky as he yanked at his clothes with brutal disregard for their value. The tension in his cheeks pulled his mouth into a grim line, but his eyes were like blazing coals, singeing her skin as he raked his gaze over her.

"Look what you do to me," he said, kicking away the last of his clothes to stand before her naked and proud. His muscled frame was pure power, the thrust of his erection stunningly potent. He worked his hands into fists that he loosened and gripped, his control visibly tenuous.

Awed, Lauren slowly swung her feet to the floor, but remained sitting on the edge of the bed. With a bold suggestiveness she had never imagined herself capable of, she spaced her wicked shoes far enough apart to open her knees and motioned him closer, eyes on the proof that he wanted her beyond bearing. "Come here."

"You are out of your mind if you think I can hold out for that."

She wanted to push him to the very brink. She reached out and took his hand, forcing him to step closer. Taking both his hands, she set them on her hair, murmuring, "Show me what you like." Then she circled her fingers around the silky muscle that pulsed in anticipation.

He swore heatedly and at length, but for a few precious moments he let her drive him out of his mind until he clasped her upper arms and pulled her to her feet, kissing her with near brutal passion before pulling back and tilting his face to the ceiling, breath hissing like a steam train.

Lauren smiled as he yanked her shirt off her, his eyes nearly blind with passion. She loved it. Loved the feel of the sweat she'd lifted on his skin, the way his heart slammed in the rib cage expanding in labored breaths, the taut thighs that shook when she grazed her hand over his buttocks and down his leg.

Her own arousal was secondary and barely acknowledged until he pressed her beneath him on the bed and held himself above her to look at her nude length in a way that was undeniably proprietary.

Old shyness struck. It was full daylight, the windows only covered by a filmy white curtain. He began setting tiny kisses onto every inch of her, heating the pulse in her wrist, teasing the side of her breast, making her flood with heat when he reached the sensitive crease at the top of her thigh.

"Paolo," she murmured in a tiny protest.

"Payback is a bitch, *tesoro,*" he muttered in Italian, sliding low to take ownership of her in the most intimate way.

She shattered and before she could recover, he rose over her.

Lauren was trembling so hard she thought she'd fall apart. He was quivering like a bowstring, his eyes holding hers with the intensity of an aim on a target. His thick hardness slid against wet, welcoming tissues that parted for him and then he was invading, silk into liquid satin, moving deeper, reaching the absolute limit of penetration and filling her up with such incredible hardness that was hot and smooth and *oh*... A sense of wholeness and completion enveloped her. Joy rippled out from her center, bathing her whole body.

They both shuddered, her gasp mingling with his jagged exhale. It was too good. She couldn't hold his gaze, wanted to turn her head and close her eyes, but he murmured, "Look at me. Keep looking at me, *cara.* Let me watch you... *Si,* like that..."

He withdrew and returned and she melted. Her insides glowed and expanded and the rush of supreme pleasure was too much to bear. She wanted to throw herself into the inferno, but he held her in hard arms, controlling their movements so his slow thrusts dragged out the pleasure, making it last so they both groaned in abandon.

She couldn't hold back forever. Unrestrained whimpers escaped her, urging him on and he responded with a snarl and shift to a wilder, deeper thrust. The meltdown started for her and the instant her nails dug into the skin of his back and her spiked heels spurred his buttocks, his neck muscles stood out with strain. His movements became jerky as he claimed her with masculine aggression that pulsed with the hot power of his release. His cries were primal and as unconstrained as hers as the cataclysm enveloped them.

They buried their faces in each other's neck, clinging on as the final quakes wrung through them, convulsing their bodies.

Bliss filled Lauren, but it ended in a barb. She suspected she might love him. Always had. And it hurt.

CHAPTER ELEVEN

"HOW ARE YOU a banker, Paolo?"

Lauren's lazy, somewhat rhetorical question pulled Paolo from a state of lassitude. They'd been making love on and off for hours. Her thigh was a warm line across his waist, her breasts plump and soft against his ribs. The weight of her head numbed his shoulder, but he didn't care. At this moment he was a newlywed and everything else was a dot on the horizon.

He yawned and stretched, then snugged her back against his side, saying dryly, "My father died before I could become an astronaut. If we're going out for dinner, we need to leave soon. Shall I call to have something delivered instead?"

"Delivery sounds good, but was that a joke? About being an astronaut? I mean, I'm sure you could have done it if you wanted to. You went to all those fancy international schools so your education was first-rate and you're incredibly fit, but really? Is that something you wanted?"

"It was a childish dream. I always knew I had to step into my father's shoes."

She came up on an elbow, her kittenish sleepiness replaced by curiosity. "Did you resent that?"

Paolo skimmed a finger along her temple, smoothing back a wisp of her short hair, surprised at how easily she was bringing up the sting of his old regret. "I might have registered my frustration with a few moments of bad judgment."

Lauren's kiss-swollen lips widened into a knowing smile. "Like surfing typhoon waves in Thailand, for instance?"

"Heard about that, did you?" He made a face at the ceiling, wondering where he got the nerve to be alive after some of the stunts he'd pulled. If his child turned out like him, he didn't know what he'd do.

"Your mother seems to think you were testing your own limits, not acting out, but were you rebelling?"

He thought back to his impatience with school and its dry courses in statistics and economics, languages and political policy. They'd made his eyes cross. The only thing that had held remote interest for him had been history because at least there was action, intrigue and battles.

"Not rebelling so much as determined to live my life to the fullest. I knew my father would eventually push the mantle onto me and I didn't want any regrets. I pulled my application to the space program when he died. It was time to put away romantic notions and do what was right."

He thought he saw a flash of protest in her eyes, but she lowered her gaze, brows tugged together in consternation. After a moment of reflection she asked, "Were you angry with him for dying?"

"Yes. I thought I'd be old before I took the reins and hated the idea of being second in command for most of my life, which is another reason I wanted to make my mark elsewhere. In space even. But you never appreciate what you have until you lose it. I'd give anything to have had him breathing down my neck all this time, training me to take over."

She nodded in understanding. "I always felt cheated, not really knowing my father. That's why I was determined to spend as much time as I could with Mamie. I didn't have your ambition for making marks, though. I took a degree with the community college in French-Canadian literature of all things. Fat lot of good that did me. I hope you've grown to like your job because I can't support myself on that."

"I do," he assured her, surprised to discover it was true because he hadn't examined his feelings on the job for years. He'd been too head-down busy. "In the beginning it was almost more than I could handle. For all my schooling I wasn't prepared, and quickly developed a new respect for my father and how easy he'd made it seem. I've grown into it, though. It still challenges me—mentally, not physically, but the stakes are higher than I ever expected, affecting not just my life and family but in some cases millions of lives. That's enough to keep me focused and engaged."

"It sounds very demanding."

"Are you worried what that means for you? Don't." He touched where she was crinkling her chin into a concerned frown. "You'll make a fine banker's wife. You have poise and style and discretion. I'm more than pleased to have you at my side."

Her lips parted as though she was about to say

something, but then her brows twitched in surprised puzzlement. "Do you travel a lot?"

"Quite a lot, yes."

"And what does that mean for me?"

He hadn't given it much thought. "Well, I suppose it means you'll have some quiet days and nights. I can't take you with me. Not while you're pregnant." As for after the baby came, he'd watched his sisters take their children on the road and it required as much preparation as launching a satellite. Definitely not worth the effort for anything less than ten days.

A mask of cool tolerance slid over Lauren's features. Her smile was tight. "Not the sort of marriage I would have chosen for myself, having lived in one just like it, but it's not about me, is it? As you said, time to put away romantic notions. This is something we did for the baby."

That was the second time she'd made their marriage sound like something she'd done out of practicality. It chafed even more this time. That was *not* the only reason they had married. Was it? Reflexively, he rolled her under him, spreading her legs with the pressure of his thighs so she could feel how quickly his body readied itself for hers.

He could feel her dampness, watched a flush of anticipation bloom under the surprise that transformed her face and heard the catch in her breath.

"I keep reminding myself you're pregnant and I shouldn't make too many demands, but do you want me again, Lauren?"

It was a deliberately worded question, one she might have answered if he hadn't leaned down to fill his hands and mouth with velvet mounds and firm, jutting nipples. The cry he wrung from her was thin and far away, reassuring him how quickly she succumbed to the same passion that held him in thrall.

He wanted to thrust into her and stamp her as his for all time, but held back, making his point in a much subtler, more enduring way, playing with her nipples until she was rocking her wet center against his shaft. Then and only then did he shift so he could kiss her while removing himself from the temptation of burying himself in her, using his hand to caress her and bring her to the brink, not letting her tip as he steadily built the intensity for both of them.

She arched her breasts into his crisp chest hair, teasing him with their damp, hard tips, while her hands roamed mindlessly over him, scratching at his buttocks and urging him to take her.

Holding back nearly killed him. His skin was incinerating by the time he slid into her. Delicate inner shivering began around his erection almost immediately and he held them both still, waiting for it to pass, mercilessly smothering her groan of protest with his hard kiss.

Finally he began the serious task of claiming her flesh and senses, pushing them to the brink of mindless intensity with slow, deep thrusts. When waves of shuddering pleasure racked her, he finally abandoned control. He thrust fast and the eruption was so fierce he shouted with ragged ecstasy, body twitching in rapture.

Then he sank onto her, weak with relief as she clung to him, shaking with joy.

"Tu sei mia," he said. *You're mine.*

But later, when they were eating spaghetti by the pool in their robes, he wondered if it was true. No romantic notions. *Would she ever really be his?*

The honeymoon lasted until New Year. Aside from a few mornings when Paolo went into his office in Milan, they were almost constantly together. They shopped for the children, sent gifts to her mother and step-nieces and nephews, and spent time with his family. There were only two awkward hiccups.

The first happened immediately after they returned from Sicily. Champagne was opened the moment they arrived at his mother's for a big family dinner. When someone handed her a glass, Lauren was caught off guard enough to hesitate before taking it, her mind teetering through the implications of refusing against taking a few sips that probably wouldn't hurt the baby.

"Thanks, but we're expecting," Paolo said smoothly, his arm curling warmly across her back. "Celebrating, but not with drink."

Into the startled silence, Vittorio drawled, "Only one day home from his honeymoon. Works fast, doesn't he?"

The blunt reminder of their indiscretion in Charleston made Lauren's heart drop, but quick as a whip, Paolo said, "Pressure's off me now. When are you going to marry and produce?"

"I keep asking him that," Paolo's aunt, Vittorio's mother, exclaimed as she came forward to offer Lauren a kiss. "Vito doesn't have your sense of duty, Paolo."

Paolo bent to hug her, smirking privately as a

din of echoed badgering was aimed at Vittorio. Vittorio ruefully muttered, *"Bastardo,"* at Paolo before embracing Lauren.

"Keep him in line, would you?" he urged her.

With everything in the open, Lauren relaxed. She and Paolo entertained at both the penthouse and the lake and ate at a restaurant where Paolo introduced her to some of his friends and their wives. It was all very festive and fun.

The second blip came when they were opening Christmas presents at his mother's. Amid the chaos of music and crumpled paper and toys being tried out, Paolo's mother said, "I suppose next year I'll be visiting you here for Baby's first Christmas."

The croon of a Christmas carol filled the sudden silence. All eyes shifted to Paolo, Lauren's included. She had no intention of turning his mother out of her home.

"Is that really what you want, Mama? Because Lauren and I are quite comfortable as we are," he said calmly.

"You can't raise a family in a skyscraper. Children need room to run and play and this house needs little feet in it full-time, not just at Christmas."

"But we don't want to displace you," Lauren

blurted. "If the house is too much for you, we can move in and you could live here with us."

"You have the heart of a true daughter, Lauren," Carlotta said with a misty smile. "Thank you, but no. I'll be happy to stay a few weeks when the baby comes if you like, but you and Paolo will want your privacy until then. And I want to be in my gardens in Tuscany. I've always wanted more time there and now I can have it."

"Don't do anything rash," Lauren urged. "Paolo's right. We're happy as we are. We have the lake house and the baby won't be walking for a year."

Carlotta seemed determined, though, and later took Lauren up to show her the nursery, suggesting Lauren start shopping to update it. Lauren reiterated that she was in no hurry, but couldn't help feeling a tingle of excitement.

Putting the baby's room together was another step toward her dream of a real family—although the part where her husband came home every night had certainly been shot down dead.

She tried not to take personally how blasé Paolo had been about traveling and leaving her at home. His position was more than a job. She understood that, but it would have been nice to see some regret. She'd had to remind herself that this was an arrangement for their child. Love and other trimmings would have to wait…if they came at all.

Nevertheless, a gaping hole opened in her every time she faced that she didn't have his heart. The constant physical attention of the first weeks of their marriage was a seductive illusion, fooling her into thinking he was growing to care for her. No matter how often they came together, they didn't seem to tire of each other, constantly finding new ways to bring forth the near violent release they were able to pull from each other. Afterward, exhausted and calmed by release, they slept tangled in a Gordian knot of bliss.

But he left, nevertheless, his mood matter-of-fact and withdrawn as he kissed her cheek and murmured something about her going into the city if she didn't want to stay at the lake house alone.

This throwback to the distant coolness he'd shown her while she was married to Ryan was a slice of sheer hell. Lauren had thought they were past that. She had thought it had had its source in jealousy and his need to control his attraction to her.

Not wanting to come across as the needy, insecure wife begging for affection, she behaved with well-trained equanimity. She knew how to swallow a fuss. Protesting or pleading that she would miss him wouldn't make a difference. Her feelings wouldn't change anything.

If you can't change your situation, change your attitude, she told herself.

But the loneliness took a toll as his schedule grew heavier. She found herself falling into old patterns of introversion, feeling isolated in this new country where Paolo's family got back to their own lives once the New Year took hold.

It was especially uncomfortable when Paolo called her over the tablet. She might tell him about a doctor appointment or the latest chapter in the pregnancy book, but she had very little to say. He was often surly and impatient, blaming mishaps in his day.

The one thing she did look forward to filling her time with was refitting the nursery, but when she dropped by to see his mother and take some measurements, she found the room completely redecorated.

It was gorgeous, freshly painted in dusky heritage colors with a parade of baby animals inching along the baseboards. Cradle, crib and change table were in place along with a rocker and daybed. Diapers, sleepers, and receiving blankets were in the drawers and the mobile played *"Frère Jacques."*

Lauren loved it at once, but had to fight revealing to Carlotta that the sight nearly pushed her to tears. What was she supposed to do for the next eighteen weeks if not daydream about a baby while organizing its nursery?

"Did you know the nursery was being done?" she asked Paolo over their evening screen time.

"Is it finished? Good." He was signing papers as he spoke, giving her only half his attention.

"So you did know," Lauren said.

"Did I not mention I'd asked Marie for a list of the best suppliers for baby furniture?"

"Because her husband had done all the research for safety standards. Yes, you said that, but you didn't say you were going to buy everything on the list and have the room painted and everything. I thought I was going to do that."

"You can't paint." He finally looked at her and even through the glass he could make her pulse trip. That made her even more quarrelsome.

"I could have decided the colors."

"You don't like them? I used the same decorator who did the lake house and you've said more than once you like what she's done there."

"That's not the point," Lauren said, feeling a buildup of familiar frustration. "Oh, forget it. Fighting long distance is a waste of time."

"Something you know from experience?" he asked with a surprisingly icy edge on his tone.

It took her aback, making her retreat even further into herself.

"Fighting at all is a waste of time," she said, trying for neutral but aware of something in her deflating. The legacy of a military wife: if this was the last time she would speak to him, did she want it to be in anger? No.

Then he would come home and she wouldn't want to rock the boat with a fight then, either. *Be a good girl, Lauren. Don't make waves.*

Her heart felt as though it would crack right open. This wasn't the dream she had envisioned for herself! She hated that she was falling into the pattern of measuring her life by her husband's comings and goings. Not that she didn't spring to life when he walked in the door. Her body began tingling just knowing he was on his way home.

By the time he arrived, they couldn't get to the bed fast enough, barely speaking, insatiable. Then they'd laze about, saying nothing until she'd work up the courage to ask when he was leaving again because the only thing worse than knowing was not knowing.

A nameless tension would come between them at that point and would linger until he left again. She didn't think he was cheating and the absences weren't that long, usually only a few days, but she dreaded them. She felt so bereft. She didn't even have to ensure his laundry was done or his toiletries were in order. He had residences all over the world and people who sent his suits for dry cleaning and recharged his shaver when necessary.

"I need a life," she wailed to the empty kitchen one morning after he'd left. She could blame Paolo all she wanted for leaving her at a loose end, but the dissatisfaction and pining were not his doing. She'd married a man who didn't love her and put herself right back into the position she'd been in when Mamie had died.

Lauren reflected on that. She had been on the brink of taking control of her life before Paolo had derailed her. Soon her baby would fill her days with diaper changes and feeding schedules and she'd be too tired to make love. Paolo's sexual crush would cool to ambivalence and then what?

Her dream of a nuclear family would implode.

Swallowing back tears that seemed to be right under the surface these days, Lauren shook off her melancholy and reminded herself why she'd come to Italy: to find family.

Heartened by the thought of doing something strictly for herself, she dug back into the few clues she had to the man's identity. A message left with one of her grandmother's oldest friends resulted in a surprise invitation a few days later to meet for dinner. Since Paolo wasn't due home for another day, Lauren accepted and began packing a bag.

Paolo was beginning to loathe business trips. At one time they had energized him, but now the slightest delay or oversight fouled his mood. Anything that created more time away from Milan grated on him.

His childhood of bouncing from country to country and school to school began to make sense. His father had spent months at a time building the bank's reputation globally. Given how his father had felt about his mother, it was no wonder the whole family had been carted along. All those fresh starts that his father had sworn to Paolo would build character were explained: Gino hadn't wanted to sleep alone.

Paolo hated it, too.

He could almost hear Ryan snickering at the depth of Paolo's fall into domesticity. The irony wasn't lost on him that Ryan had never exhibited the same eagerness to rush home to the exact same woman.

Nor was it lost on him that Lauren had complained more than once about her first husband's absences, but seemed almost anxious to get rid of her second, asking Paolo practically the minute he was in the door when he'd be leaving next.

It didn't help that he was doubling up on his overseas duties, trying to square away as much as possible and delegate responsibilities so he could take time when the baby came. He felt like a schoolboy watching the clock, waiting for the bell that would release him into his life outside these walls, where Lauren and their baby were waiting.

An abrupt cancellation of a meeting by a European Union representative allowed him to leave

Zurich at noon, rather than waiting until the morning. Paolo frowned at the nearly visceral relief from pain. What was happening to him?

He brushed past the flight attendant in his own jet and had to fight the urge to enter the cockpit. He shouldn't be so agitated that he wanted to take up old coping strategies, but waiting to be *taken* to Lauren felt intolerable. He wanted to pilot his return to her at his own agitated speed, pushing where possible and landing in record time before opening up the engine of his sports car full throttle to the lake house.

He made himself hold back, determined not to regress into that impetuous young man who'd taken too many chances because he couldn't contain his emotions. Intense feelings that he'd managed to tamp down for years had been flaring up ever since Lauren had sashayed back into his life. *That* was intolerable.

He pushed his finger and thumb into his eye sockets, pinching the bridge of his nose and reaching for patience. What he felt for Lauren was completely uncontrollable. The more he fought it, the worse it got.

Silently resolving to master himself, he held to

his typical land speed of merely outrageous rather than testing the true limits of the car's engine. That might denote desperation and he wasn't quite there yet. He told himself.

To his surprise, Lauren was in the entryway shrugging a jacket over her shoulders. She froze as he entered. She had her boots on and an overnight bag at her feet, but a startled flash-fire of joy overrode her initial shock, sending a kick of emotion into his gut. The apprehension he'd been nursing fell away.

"I was going to email you and tell you to meet me at the penthouse. I thought you said you'd be home tomorrow." She came forward to greet him with a kiss full of sensuous welcome. Her weight tilted into him so her bump nudged his stomach.

He wove his fingers into the warm strands of her hair, unable to stop himself from keeping her close so he could feast on her supple lips. *Dio!* It felt like it had been months.

When she broke away, her face shone with excitement. "This works, too. We can drive in together," she said breathlessly.

"I just got here." He set his keys on the table so

he could properly pull her close and absorb the feel of her. His equilibrium began to balance out.

"Yes, but—"

Paolo cut her off, kissing her with the hungry insistence that always melted her bones. Lauren was tempted. He ignited her blood, every time. But it was exactly that sensation of coming to life after days of flatness that made her draw back.

"I'm meeting someone," she told him, and explained about reaching the woman who had known the man her grandmother had been seeing.

Paolo frowned. "Surely you can put that off?"

Lauren carefully extricated herself from Paolo's firm grip. He looked drained and tired and she felt herself softening, but what happened the next time and the next? She *had* to start standing up for what she wanted. If he loved her, it might be different, but given the state of their marriage, she needed to establish emotional independence.

"I could," she conceded, aware of crumpled hope sitting like litter in her heart. "But why should I?"

"Because your husband arrived home early and you'd prefer to catch up with him since he'll be gone again later this week. She'll understand and reschedule, I'm sure."

Well, that answered that question. Lauren's face hurt, trying not to react. She stared at the wall, already suffering the quiet desperation of his next absence. Something had to change. She had to fill her life with more than pining for her husband.

"I don't want to wait," she said tonelessly.

Paolo's hands dropped away. "No? Perhaps I should have stayed in Switzerland then."

"I thought you *were* staying in Switzerland. That's why I made plans. When you make plans, do I get in the way of them?" she challenged.

"I'm well aware you don't give a damn if I'm here or not, Lauren."

"I never said that!" Her lungs felt as though glass dust poofed into them, but she couldn't bring herself to pour out how forlorn she was without him. "Just because I know how to live around a man's schedule doesn't mean—"

"Stop throwing him in my face," he cut in.

She jerked her head back. He had a very tight rein on his temper, she realized, and it ignited hers.

"Is that what I'm doing?" she asked shakily. "Because I thought I was explaining that after a lifetime of going along with everyone else, I'm taking one evening for myself. Which I invited you to come along on, but I'm retracting that. If you want to join me in Milan, you can follow in your own car."

She shouldered her bag, shaking with anger that was a precious cover for the hurt that was crippling up her insides. He really did only want a bedmate not a lifemate.

"Don't hold your breath, *cara,*" he said scornfully.

"Oh, I won't. I'm equally aware that I don't mean a damn thing to you beyond a sex partner and a vessel for your child." So vulnerable she felt naked, she asked, "What do you want, Paolo? A wife who wheedles and begs for your affection? One who makes her husband the source of her self-esteem and happiness? You don't want that burden any more than Ryan did and my pride won't let me sink to those depths again."

CHAPTER TWELVE

AT LEAST IT would signify that he meant something to her, Paolo thought as she drove away. At least if she asked for his love, he'd know she wanted it.

The truth washed over him in a nuclear blast of heat and light. *He loved her.*

And like an H-bomb, the fallout left him blistered to his bones, blind and screaming silently.

Because she didn't love him back.

Paolo understood love better than most. He had a huge family he cared for with all his heart. He would fight to the death for every single one of them, including Lauren. How could he have missed that this emotion tearing him up was love?

Because for the first time it was imbued with sexual need and something stronger. A pair-bond that went deeper than blood ties. It went all the way into his soul.

As he stood there in the darkening house, he wondered how he'd let the woman he loved walk away with such a shattered look in her eyes. He'd been so wrapped up in not betraying his own hurt, he'd ignored that she had needs, too. Needs that weren't being answered because her pride was in the way and so was his.

She wouldn't beg for his affection, but did she want it?

She had it regardless. Maybe she didn't love him back, but he couldn't keep it inside himself. *Dio!* Now that he recognized what filled him, it threatened to split him open if he didn't express it.

Lauren had to pull onto a side street and have a good cry before she carried on to Milan. She thought about going back to the lake house, but honestly, what good would it do to slink back into the house with puffy eyes and a bruised heart? You couldn't force someone to love you. It was either there or it wasn't.

For her it was. Very much so.

Oh, Paolo.

Once she could see again, she carried on to Milan where she left the car with the valet of the apartment building and walked the few blocks to the restaurant. Five minutes in the ladies' room repaired her makeup, but she was still fragile and emotional when she was shown to a table with not one, but two women.

The elder was her grandmother's friend Luce. The younger was introduced as Emelia. Emelia was about Lauren's age and bore a striking resemblance to photos of Lauren's mother when Lauren had been a baby. Lauren sank into her chair, amazed and overcome.

Emelia had brought a snapshot of Mamie as a young woman. "My mother stole it from my father's things. She was very bitter that her father had had an affair."

"I wish I had remembered to charge my phone in the car so I could show you photos of my mother. I take after my grandmother, but you and Mom obviously take after our grandfather."

They both smiled with pained fatalism as they concluded that neither of their mothers was likely to pursue this family connection. Oddly, that formed a bond of kinship between Lauren and Emelia that Lauren instinctively knew would grow over time. They took each other's details and promised to be in touch.

As gratifying as meeting her half cousin was,

however, Lauren knew it could have waited. She hadn't needed to be so stubborn about it. As she strolled her way back to the Donatelli Tower and entered the elevator to the penthouse, she had to fight a resurgence of tears. She shouldn't have argued with Paolo. The upside to being a doormat was never making anything worse than it already was. She'd just learned that the hard way.

But she supposed the problems in their marriage would have come to a head anyway. She just wished she knew how they were going to work it out. No matter how hopeless it seemed, they had to. They had a baby on the way.

Which meant she'd be groveling, and that made her teeth clench in protest.

The elevator pinged and the doors opened. Paolo stood on the other side, his Italian heritage in full display with an undertone of darkness to his skin, his eyes blazing with passionate emotion. "Where the hell have you been?"

Lauren fell back a step, stunned. He still wore his rumpled clothes. His face was lined with fatigue and something else that made a fierce white light strike through her as he raked his gaze over her, pulling her apart.

"I told you, I had a dinner date." She skittishly exited the elevator.

"Where? I left right after you did, but I didn't pass you. I was watching for you. How fast were you driving, Lauren?"

She let him take the weight of her bag and side-stepped his intimidating nearness. "I pulled off to use the ladies' room and need to again," she excused, anxious to drag her composure together. What was he *doing* here? Her body shook with re-action while her mind raced. She wanted to take this as a good sign, but a sign of what? *Did* he want some needy pushover of a wife?

"Why didn't you answer your mobile?" he demanded the minute she emerged.

"It needs to be charged," she said, drying her still-damp palms on her backside before finding the phone in her purse. She walked it to the dock in the corner.

Had she really been wishing he had come with her? Right now his dynamic presence made her feel like her world was crashing in. If she was still sometimes overwhelmed by the effect he had on her physically, at least she was used to it, but there was a fresh intensity to him that seemed like a lasso swirling above her head, waiting to alight around her and yank her in. It made her wary because she knew if it happened, she was done. There'd be no self-protection left.

"What, um, changed your mind about coming?" she hazarded to ask.

"I wanted to know something." He scowled at the way she circled away from him toward the windows on the far side of the sofa. She could see his reflection, arms folding with dismay.

Not sex, then, and definitely not because he missed her. Lauren looked at her feet, then lifted her head. The view of Milan was a blanket of sparkling lights that her blurring eyes didn't see.

"You could have called," she pointed out.

"I wanted to see your face when I asked."

"Oh, good God, it wasn't a man, Paolo." She swung around so he could see the hurt and offense on her face. "It was a friend of my grandmother's and my half cousin. Or quarter. I don't know what we are, but she was nice and I'm happy I met her. Okay?"

"Of course it wasn't a man. Because you love me, don't you?"

She sucked in a pained breath, feeling tricked

into turning around and letting him see what a devastating effect his question had on her. She couldn't hide the truth, not from him. That sort of dissembling had been peeled away layer by layer over the past weeks of intense physical closeness.

It seemed an especially nasty betrayal that he just stood there staring at her, silently demanding the truth from her. Demanding she bare her soul. Insisting she reveal what she wanted most in this world so he could tell her she couldn't have it.

Well, damn him anyway.

"Yes," she declared with a hint of defiance and tried to stare him down, but her brows were twitching and her inner barriers quivering under the onslaught of intense feelings she couldn't contain.

He was far better at it than her, penetrating into her psyche with a look that burned all the way from across the room.

"How long have you loved me?"

She couldn't help flinching. His voice was almost tender, but the question was so cruel she could hardly bear it.

"I don't know." She realized she couldn't think of a time when she hadn't loved him. When his opinion hadn't mattered. When his attention hadn't scored her like a knife. When every cell in her being hadn't been tuned in to him. Her lips trembled and her body convulsed in a shivering shrug. "Forever?"

"Then why in hell did you marry Ryan?" he asked in a voice that cracked.

She flinched, possibly able to withstand contemptuous fury but he sounded *hurt*.

"I was young and stupid," she said defensively, rallying with a pained, "You know what that's like. You did the same thing. You married that other woman."

"She wasn't anyone you knew. I didn't flaunt her under your nose for five damned *years!*"

So harshly unforgiving she wanted to cry, but how could she have known it mattered? How?

Paolo could only imagine what he looked like. His hands had been spiking up his hair for the last two hours while he waited for her, getting nothing but voice mail until he was convinced she was in a ditch somewhere.

"I hated you for that, Lauren," he admitted, finally getting off his chest a weight that had been suffocating him unacknowledged since forever.

She made a sound of extreme hurt, giving him

a pinch of compunction, but this particular wound needed flushing before it would close and heal.

"You married the wrong man."

It wasn't anything she hadn't said to herself, but the way he said it, angry and filled with accusation, was new and freshly hurtful.

"You think I should have left my wedding with you." It was completely illogical, so much easier to say than it would have been to do, but in her heart she believed it, too.

"Yes," he agreed, a ring of accusation still in his voice.

"I didn't think you were serious. I *believed* you hated me." Her voice cracked and she couldn't continue. Her hands ached where she clutched them together and she tried again to focus on the Milan skyline, but to no avail. The wall of windows was a black slate with a single lamp reflected in it. It winked as Paolo passed in front of it and came to stand behind her and grasp her shoulders.

She ducked her head, devastated anew by his power to hurt her with nothing but his own hurt.

"What I feel for you isn't love, Lauren."

A paroxysm of pure anguish struck her. Before

she could recoil, his hands tightened and he spoke with swift intensity.

"Love is a security blanket your family gives you. It makes you strong enough to take on the world. You are not a warm, fuzzy blanket, Lauren. You're a wildfire. You're a drop out of a plane without a chute. What I feel for you makes me feel weak and scared and *I can't control it.* I have conquered a million different challenges and the one thing I couldn't do was stop what I felt for you, even though it could destroy lives."

She lifted her head and turned to search his eyes, drawn on a rack of conflicting beliefs.

Paolo framed her face with gentle hands. "What I feel for you is so much bigger than love. You struck me between the eyes the first time I saw you, so much so that I drank myself into oblivion that night. I didn't put it together. I didn't realize that the reason I was so gutted by that baby not being mine was because I'd given up something precious for it. *You.*"

"I didn't think it mattered who I married because the one man who intrigued me was taken," she confided, seeing that truth now.

"I should have stolen you from the church before you went down the aisle. These lonely years for both of us have been my fault," he said bleakly.

She touched his lips, fingertips dampened by his hot breath as delicate hope invaded her heart. "You had to straighten out the bank. I needed to grow up. Mamie needed me. Perhaps it worked out as it was meant to."

He nodded somberly. "But I would have come to you in Charleston even if you hadn't called. It might have been a day or two later, after his death was made public, but nothing would have kept me away. Nothing would be different now."

"We'd still have had that fight this evening before leaving the house?" she teased, tearing up with remembered hurt, but soothing over it for both of them.

He smirked ruefully. "Probably. Because when a man loves a woman this much, he can't believe she's so obtuse about what it means when he rushes home to see her."

"But that's because I'm not—"

He kissed her, stilling any self-deprecating argument she might have raised.

Paolo lifted his head a few minutes later. A light she'd never seen shone from his eyes. "Quit telling me what you're not. You're a Donatelli. That puts you head and shoulders above the rest right there."

His arrogance made her smile, which only made him stand taller and even more proud. "You're gloriously human, Lauren. Passionate and softhearted and capable of making mistakes because you love someone. I need that, working with numbers and bankers and economists all day."

"Exactly. Human. Not an international space station or anything really exciting."

"And yet I feel omnipotent, having won your love."

She blinked fast, trying to see through her tears. "What I feel for you…" She bit her lip. "I always knew you had the power to consume me. I was afraid to let you, afraid of how intense my feelings were. I never felt this way with Ryan."

He cupped her face, thumbs gently smoothing under her damp eyes. "I used to think that after the childhood he'd had, he deserved the love of a good woman. It's the only way I could justify not stealing you from him. It's his loss that he didn't appreciate you, Lauren. I won't make that mistake."

Her smile trembled and fell apart under his tender kiss. Slowly they melted into each other, for once savoring their reunion because they knew now, without doubt, that they had the rest of their lives together.

EPILOGUE

Fourteen weeks later...

LAUREN SMILED, FEELING as though she was an actor in a movie. The hee-haw of the ambulance siren was so European.

"There's nothing funny about this, Lauren." Paolo took the oxygen mask off his face to speak, rocking on his seat as the ambulance took a sharp corner.

"Don't be angry at me. This is the one who didn't want to wait for the ambulance." She pointed at the sleeping infant swaddled beside her, his little face screwed up in a masculine frown of concentration, as though everything he did would be done intensely whether it be sleep, cry or deliver.

No mystery where he'd get a quality like that from, Lauren thought with another affectionate grin.

"He and I will have words about this, make no

mistake. He almost put me into an early grave. I still feel weak," Paolo complained, his words belied by the flush of pride that shone off him like a halo.

"Keep breathing, Papa," the female attendant said, urging him to replace the oxygen mask over his mouth and nose. "Your wife did all the work, you know. Catching is the easy part."

"He did very well," Lauren defended faithfully. "But I bet you pity your parents now, don't you?"

"Quite a bit," Paolo acceded ruefully. "If this is any indication, karma has arrived in a one-stone package of heartstopping payback."

"But don't you just love him, Paolo?" Lauren pleaded. She was too new to motherhood to hear any slights against her precious son.

"I do," Paolo said with deep emotion, leaning forward to touch his son's ruddy cheek. "And I love you." He met her eyes as he said it, letting her see the depth of feeling in him, filling her with his love in a single, impactful look. "Thank you for our baby."

She blinked, touched to her core. "I love you, too."

He smiled with satisfaction, glancing at their son

again with conspiratorial good humor. "Looks like he travels well. Good thing, since we'll be doing so much of it. But no more surprises," he warned Lauren with a stern point of his finger. "The next one is planned, start to finish."

"Agreed."

Four months later they accidentally conceived on a flight to Hong Kong. Their daughter arrived three weeks early in a limousine under the Arc de Triomphe.

* * * * *

Mills & Boon® Large Print
November 2013

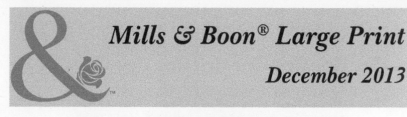

Mills & Boon® Large Print

December 2013

THE BILLIONAIRE'S TROPHY
Lynne Graham

PRINCE OF SECRETS
Lucy Monroe

A ROYAL WITHOUT RULES
Caitlin Crews

A DEAL WITH DI CAPUA
Cathy Williams

IMPRISONED BY A VOW
Annie West

DUTY AT WHAT COST?
Michelle Conder

THE RINGS THAT BIND
Michelle Smart

A MARRIAGE MADE IN ITALY
Rebecca Winters

MIRACLE IN BELLAROO CREEK
Barbara Hannay

THE COURAGE TO SAY YES
Barbara Wallace

LAST-MINUTE BRIDESMAID
Nina Harrington

1113 Rom LP